Tim & Gerald R

Summer on Grandma's Farm

Book 5 in the Tim & Gerald Ray Series

Copyright © 2024. All rights reserved.

ALL RIGHTS RESERVED: No part of this book may be reproduced,stored, or transmitted, in any form, without the express and prior permission in writing of Your New Life Ministries LLC.

This book may not be circulated n any form of binding or cover other than that in which it is currently published. This book is licensed for your personal enjoyment only. All rights are reserved.

Your New Life Ministries LLC does not grant you rights to resell or distribute this book without the prior written consent of both Your New Life Ministries LLC and the copyright owner of this book.

This book must not be copied, transferred, sold, or distributed in any way. Disclaimer: Neither Your New Life Ministries LLC nor our authors will be responsible for repercussions to anyone who utilizes the subject of this book for illegal, immoral, or unethical use.

This is a work of fiction. The views expressed herein do not necessarily reflect that of the publisher.

This book or part thereof may not be reproduced in any form, stored in a retrieval system, or transmitted in any form by any means-electronic,mechanical, photocopy, recording, or otherwise without prior written consent of the publisher, except as provided by the United States of America copyright law.

Note: Pictures are strictly models and names and places in this book in no way represent in real person or place. The places, events and people are strictly fictitious.
Second Edition
Published by: Your New Life Ministries LLC
www.yournewlifeministries.org
Published in the United States of America

**Enjoy another adventure with
Timmy and Gerald Ray.**

In Summer on Grandma's Farm, Tim and Gerald Ray are taking a trip to grandma's farm for summer break. They are not looking forward to it! To their amazement they learn about animals, gardens, get chased by a rooster and learn a lesson from God as well! Peek inside and receive an understanding of the Trinity along with the boys!

Summertime! Timmy and Gerald Ray love summertime! Instead of the usual summer vacation, they are going to grandma's farm. Mom and Dad thought it would be a good experience for them to see how farm animals are taken care of and how vegetables are grown.

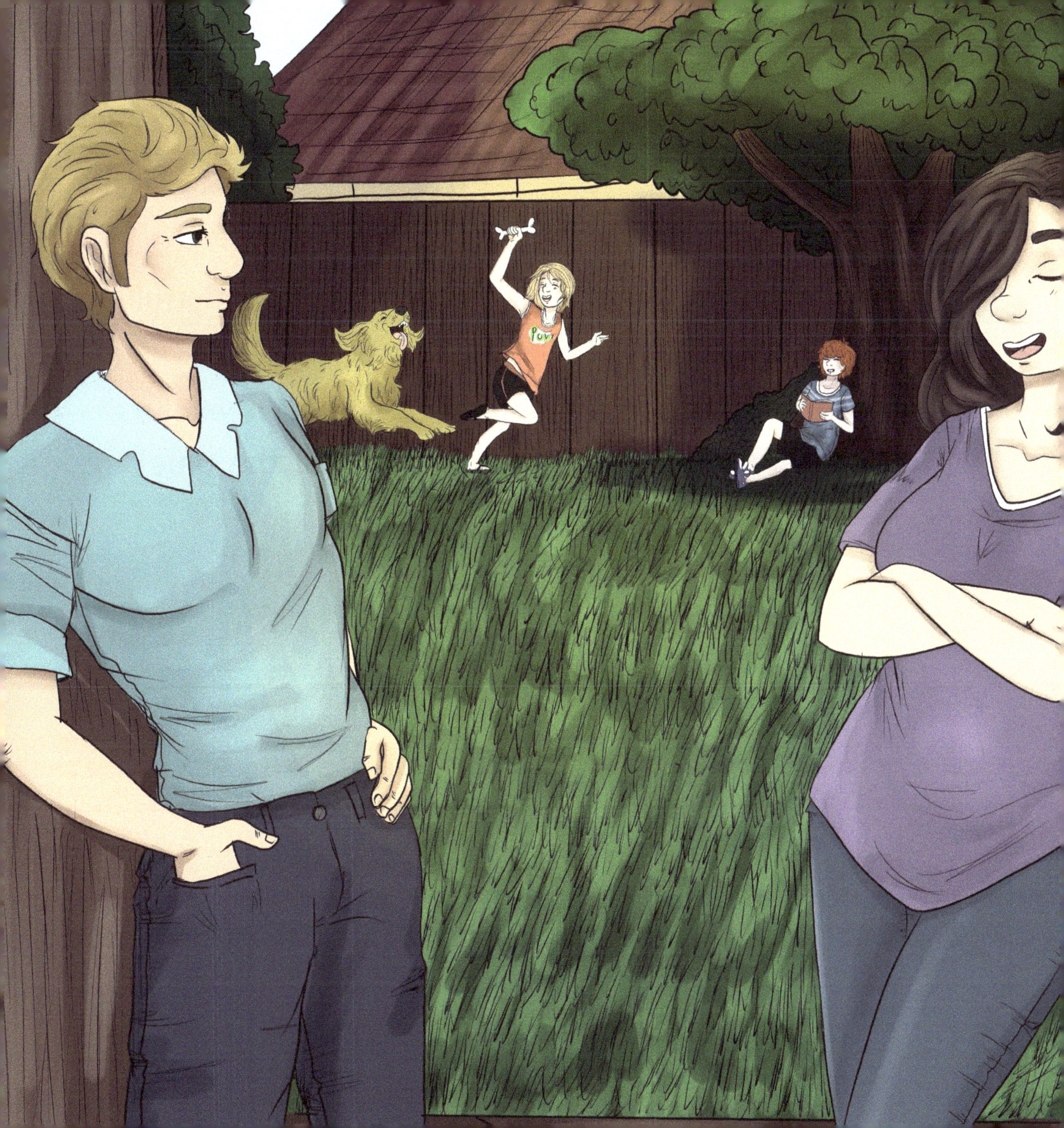

As Dad explained how they would have a wonderful time, their jaws dropped!

They replied, "Dad, we don't want to go! It will be boring! Grandma will make us work all the time! Don't make us go!"

POW

Mom stepped in, "Boys, it won't be as bad as you think. You love animals; once you are there you will have a great time! Remember grandma's dog, Scruffy? You liked him and you can even bring your fishing poles. There is a pond down the road from grandma's house."

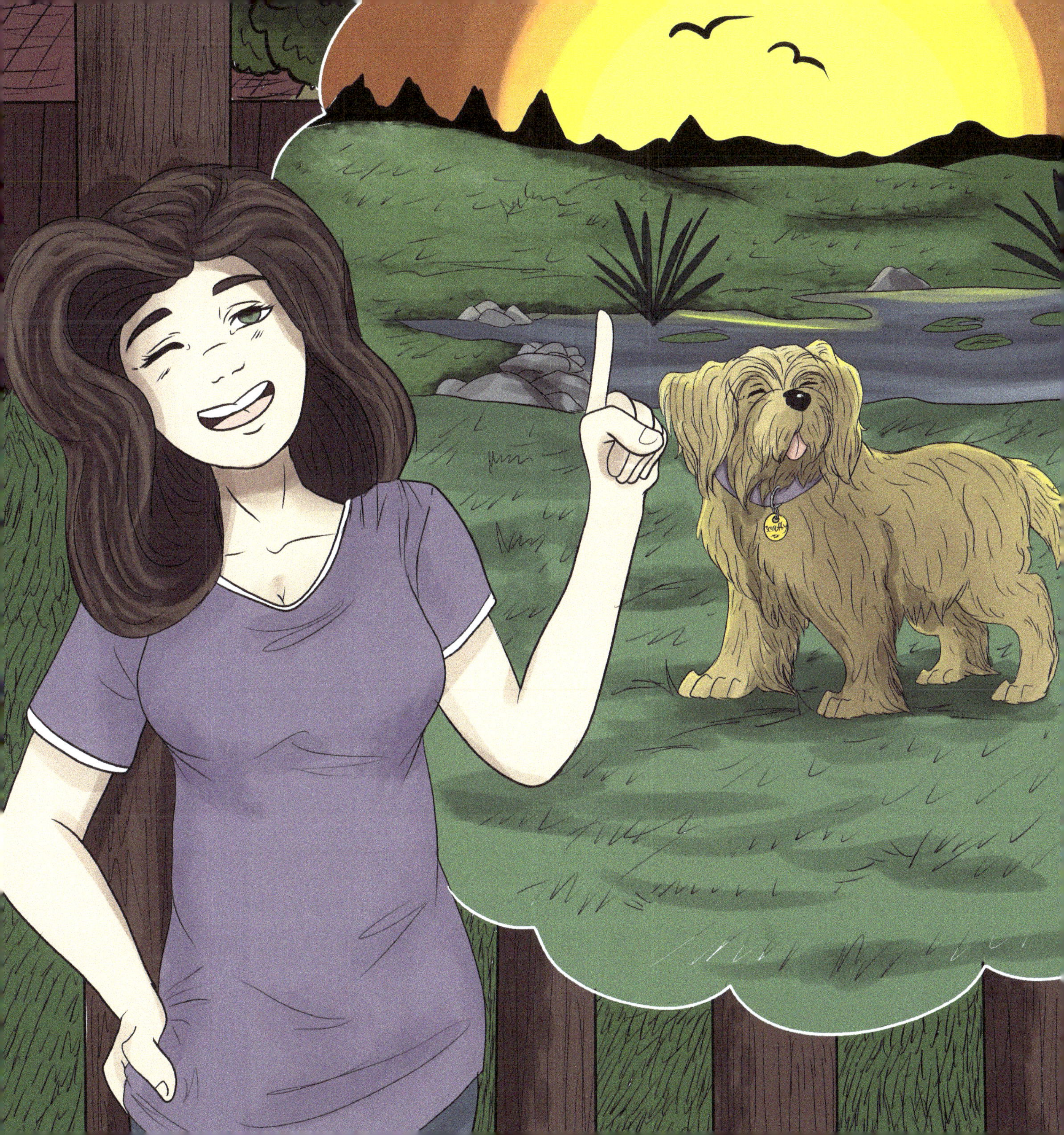

"Oh yeah," Timmy replied as the frown on his face faded away.

They talked, then went to their parents and said, as if they had a choice, "We guess it will be alright, as long as we can bring our fishing poles."

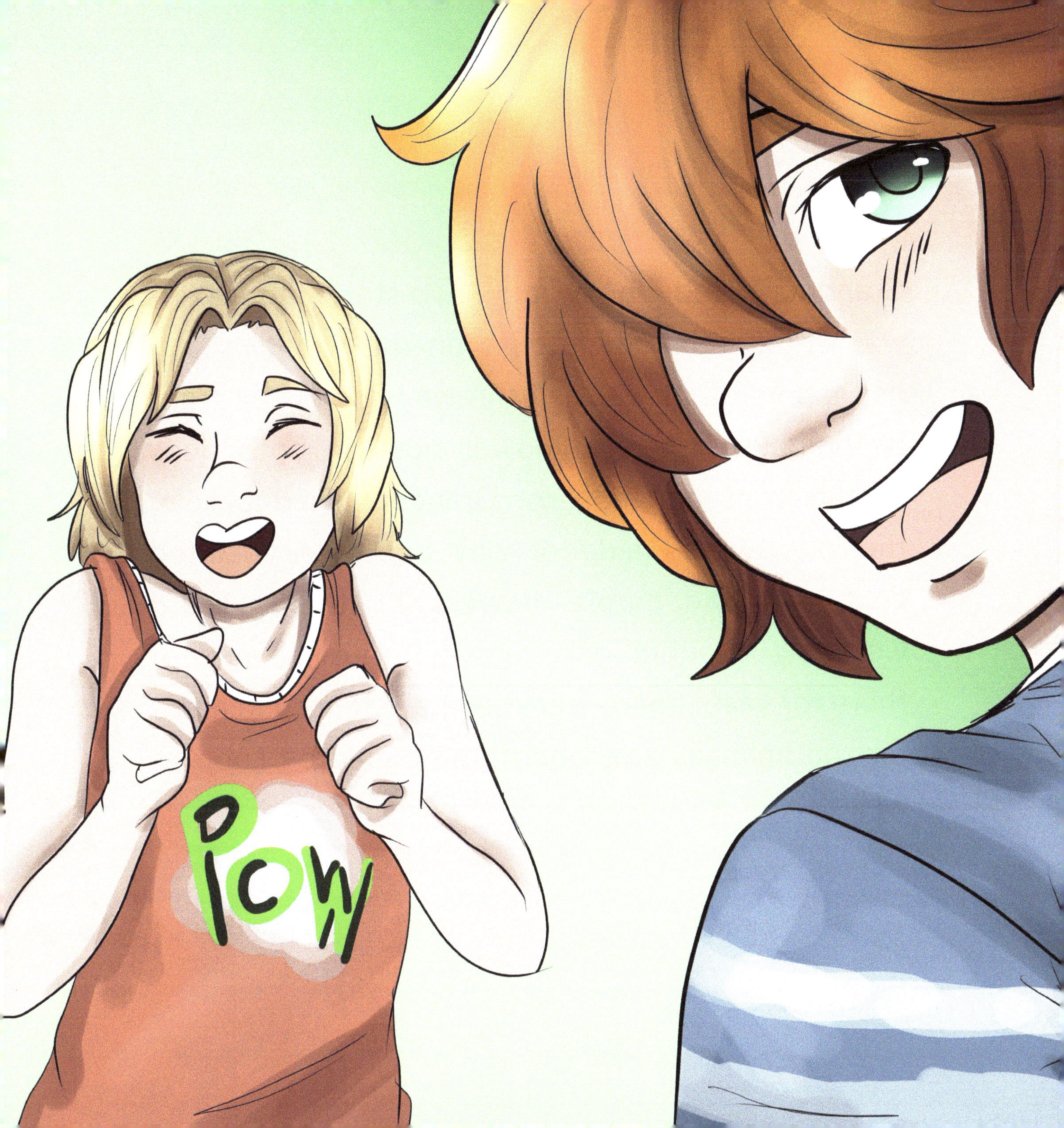
POW

Grandma lived in a big two-story house. It was white with red shutters on the windows and had a porch that went all the way across the front of the house. She had flower pots on both sides of the front porch steps. Grandma liked purple; the pots were made of clay and were painted gold, and had purple flowers in them. There were big beautiful oak trees that must have been there for years, there were separate fenced in areas for the animals, a red barn and a chicken coop as well

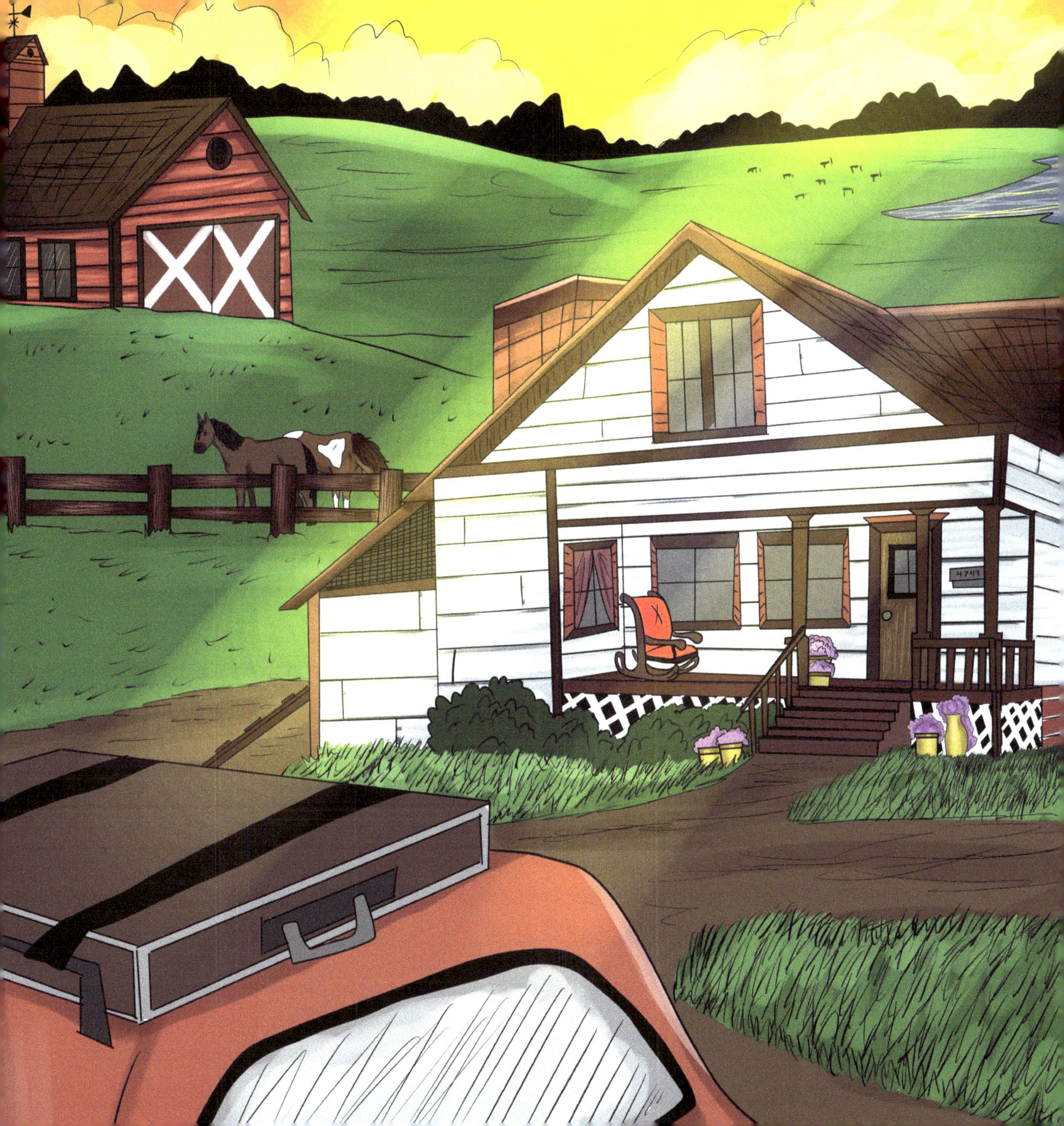

Grandma came out to meet them smiling! Looking around as they got out of the car Tim said, "Boy, Gerald Ray, the farm is bigger than I remembered. Look at the cows in the pen and look at the horses! Grandma can we ride them?"

There was a brown one and one that was white with brown spots.

"I want to ride the spotted one," Gerald Ray shouted as he ran to meet grandma.

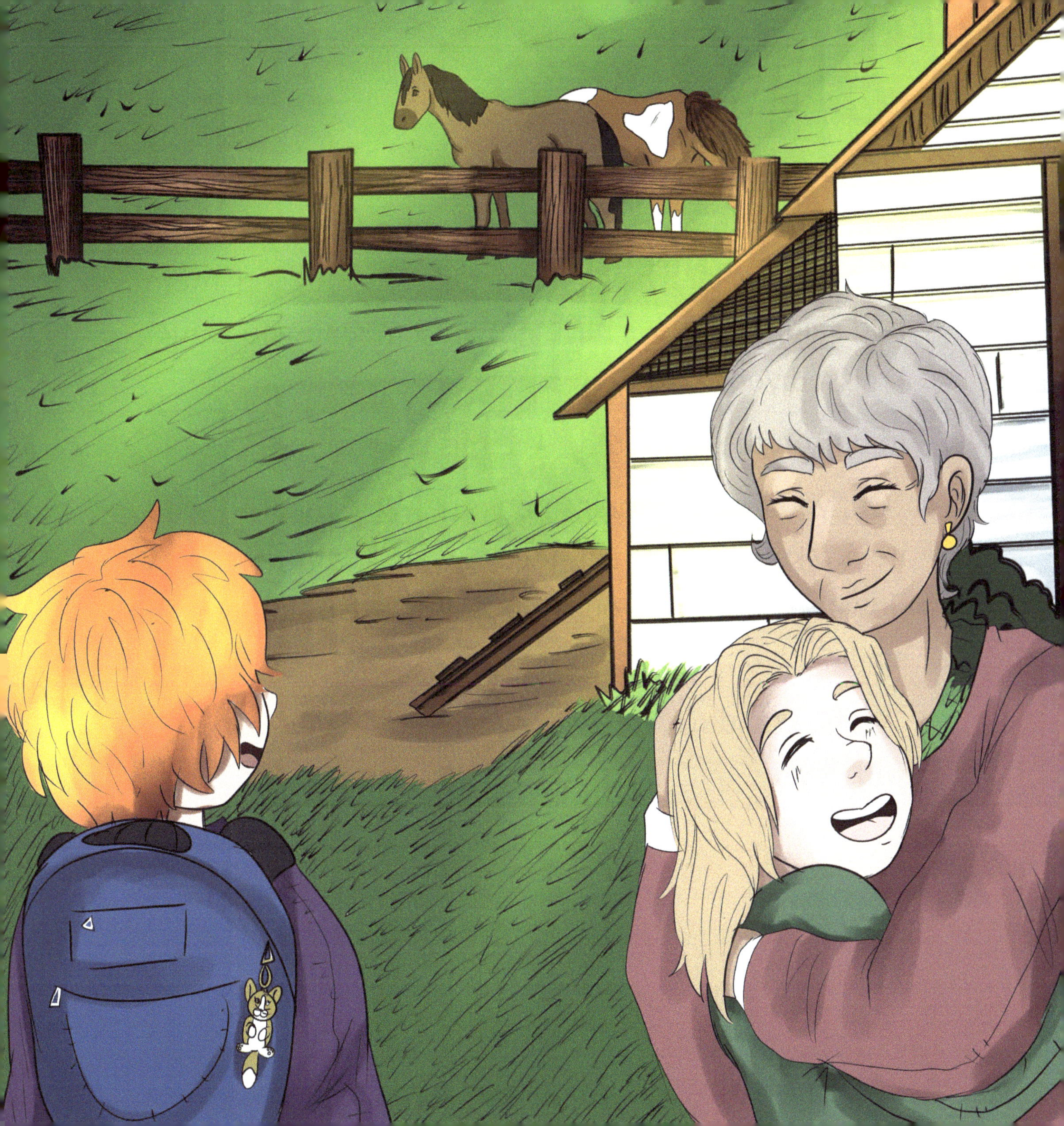

Grandma came up to the boys with Scruffy tagging along with her wagging his tail. She hugged them and said, "You boys have grown! I'm glad you came. I missed you!"

In unison they shouted, "We missed you too!"

"Oh, you like the horses do you? Well, maybe if you help take care of them, feed, water and brush them down, I will let you ride them," Grandma said smiling.

"Yeah, grandma we will, we will!" They shouted with joy!

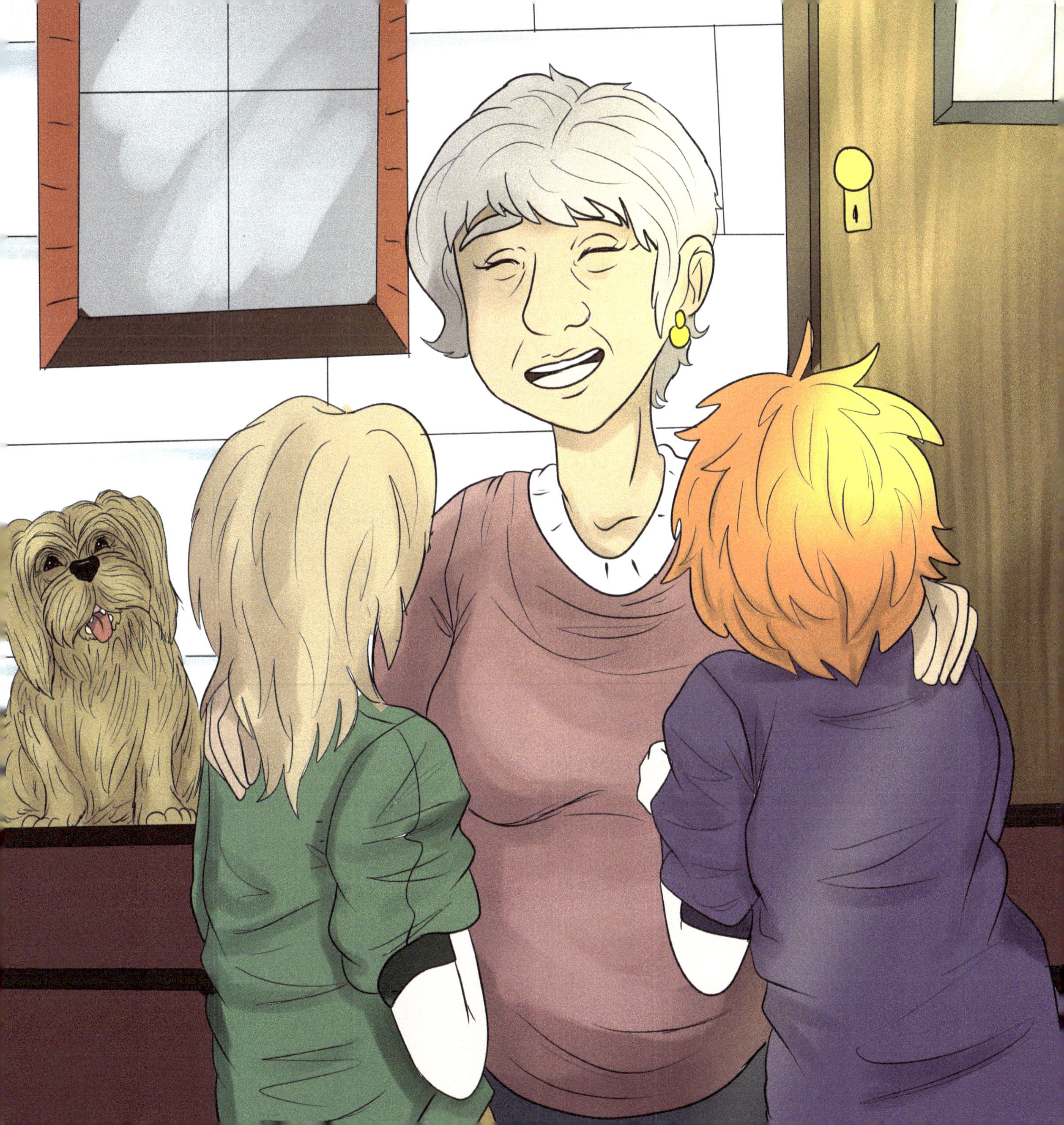

Mom came over and hugged grandma too, "Hi, Mom. I am glad to see you. I hope the boys won't be too much for you?"

Grandma looked at them and said, "Oh no, in fact, I can tell they will be a big help to me. It will not be all work and no play, but since it is just me now, this farm is a handful."

I have a hired hand, Randy, who takes care of the animals. He is a big help.

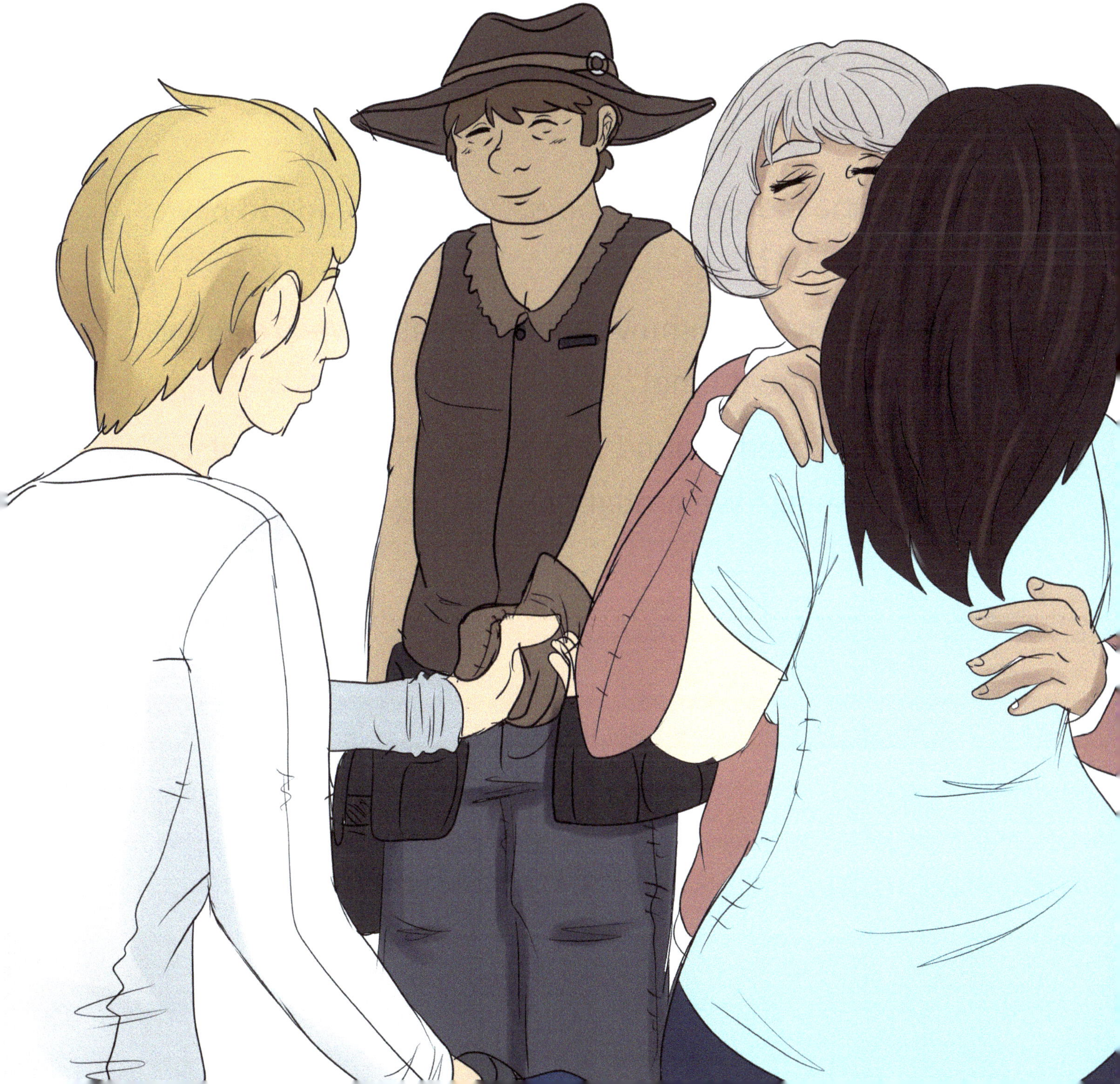

Grandma looked at the boys, "Are you ready to have a good time?"

Gerald Ray and Timmy replied, "Yeah! We are going to have a great time!"

Timmy looked around and asked, "Is there a place to go fishing? We brought our fishing poles."

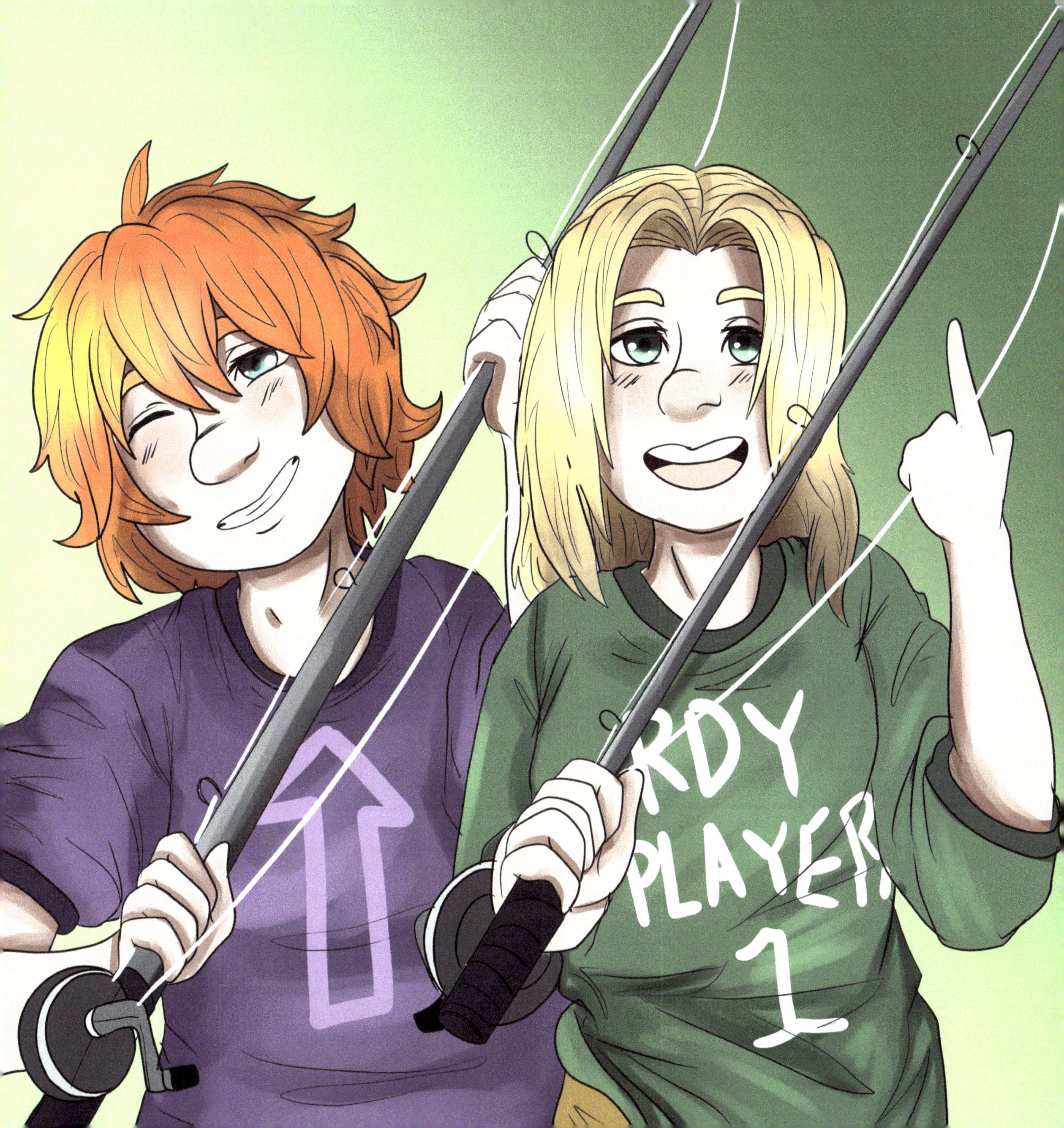
RDY
PLAYE
1

Grandma pointed across the field to the right of her house and said, "It is right past the field and down the road a piece."

"Yeah!" They shouted for joy and looked over at their parents and said, "Mom and Dad, we think we are going to like it here after all."

Dad looked over at them and with an "I told you so," he said with a big grin on his face, "I knew you would

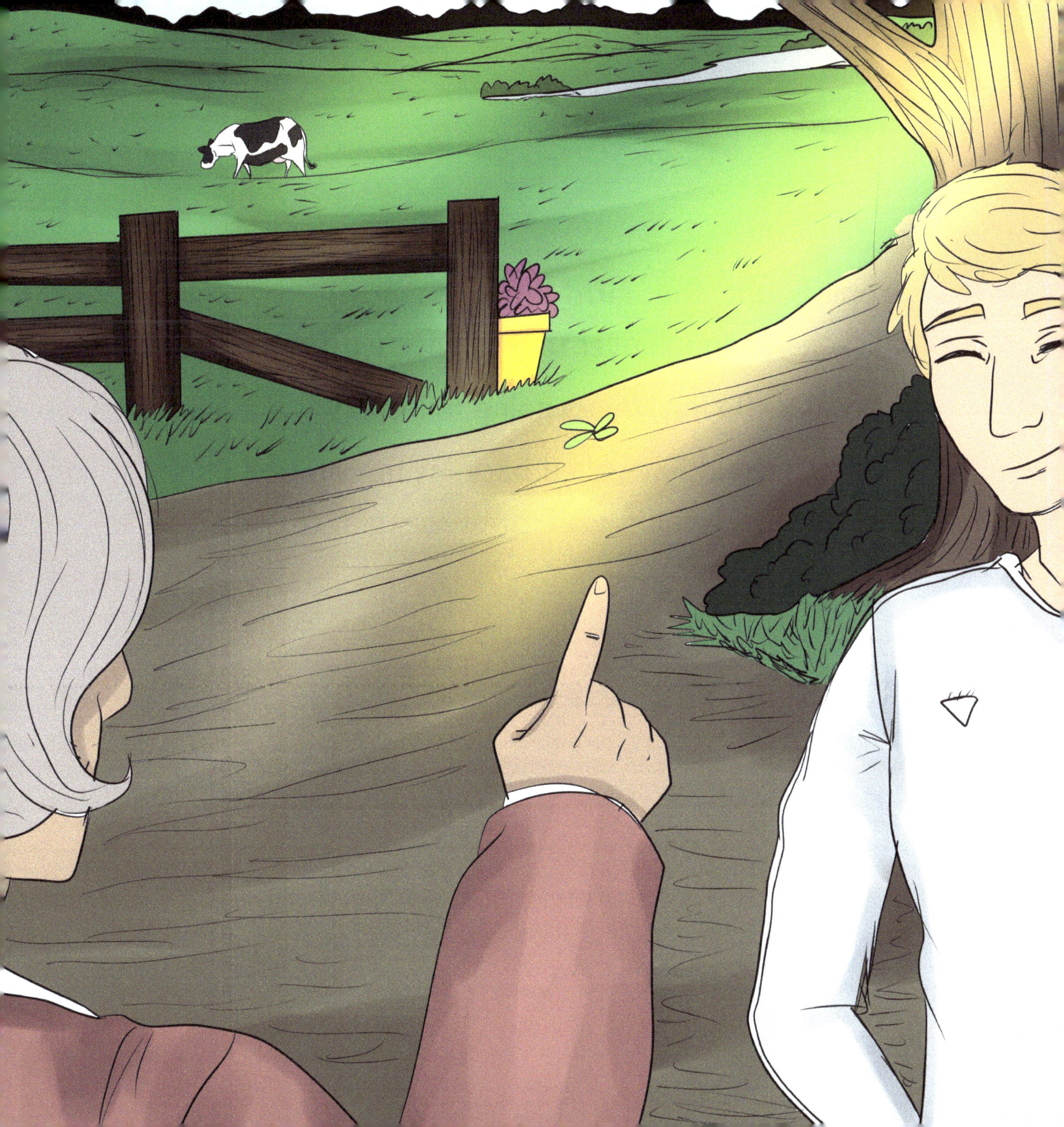

Scoping out the farm, they saw the cows and chickens, then ran over to the fence with the horses.

"Wow Gerald Ray, this is going to be fun."

"Yeah," Gerald Ray yelled back, as he climbed up on the fence, "I can't wait until we get to ride the horses!"

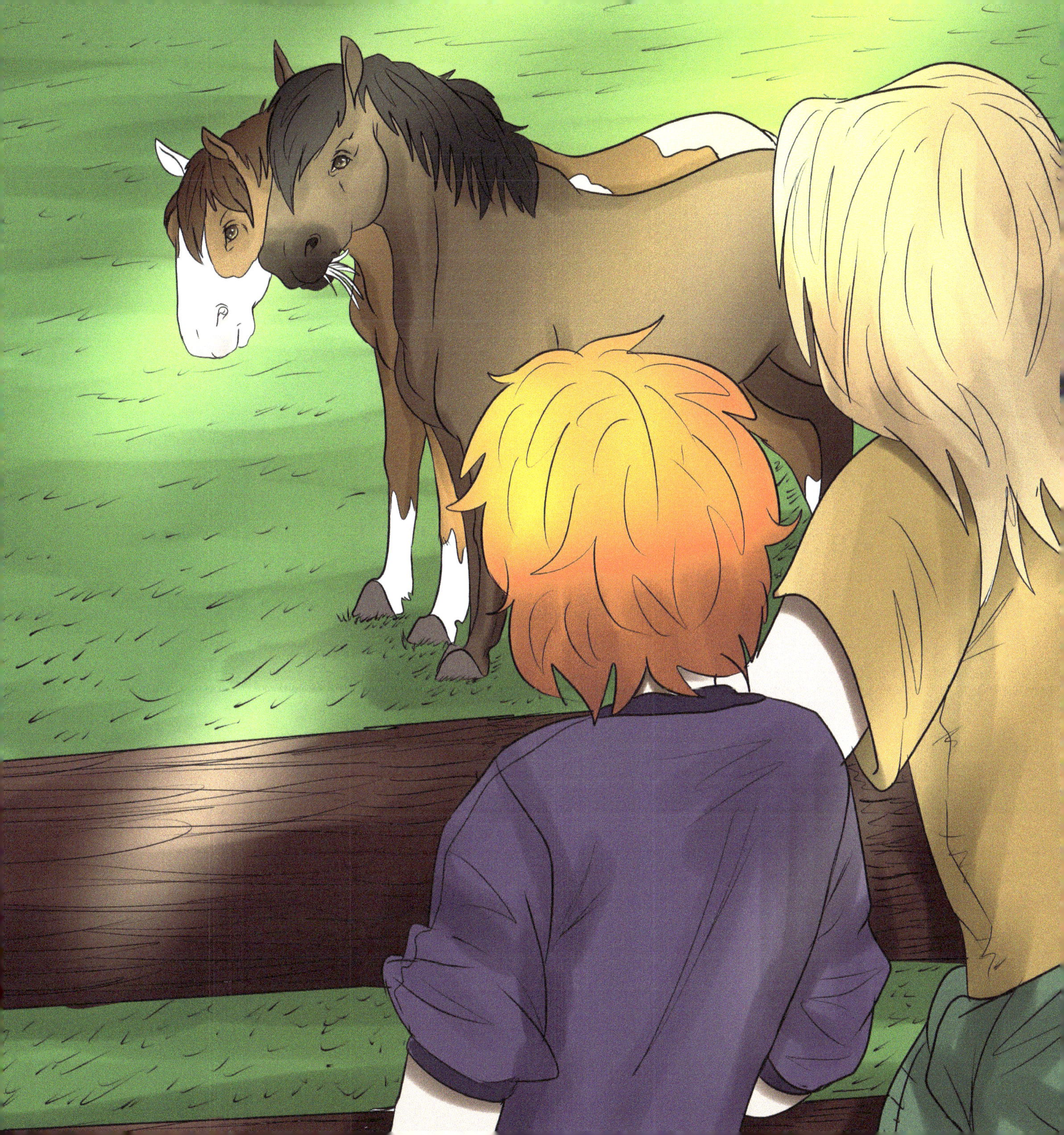

Mom came out on the porch, "Boys, it is time for dinner, grandma made fried chicken!"

They always loved grandma's fried chicken.

"We're coming," Timmy shouted.

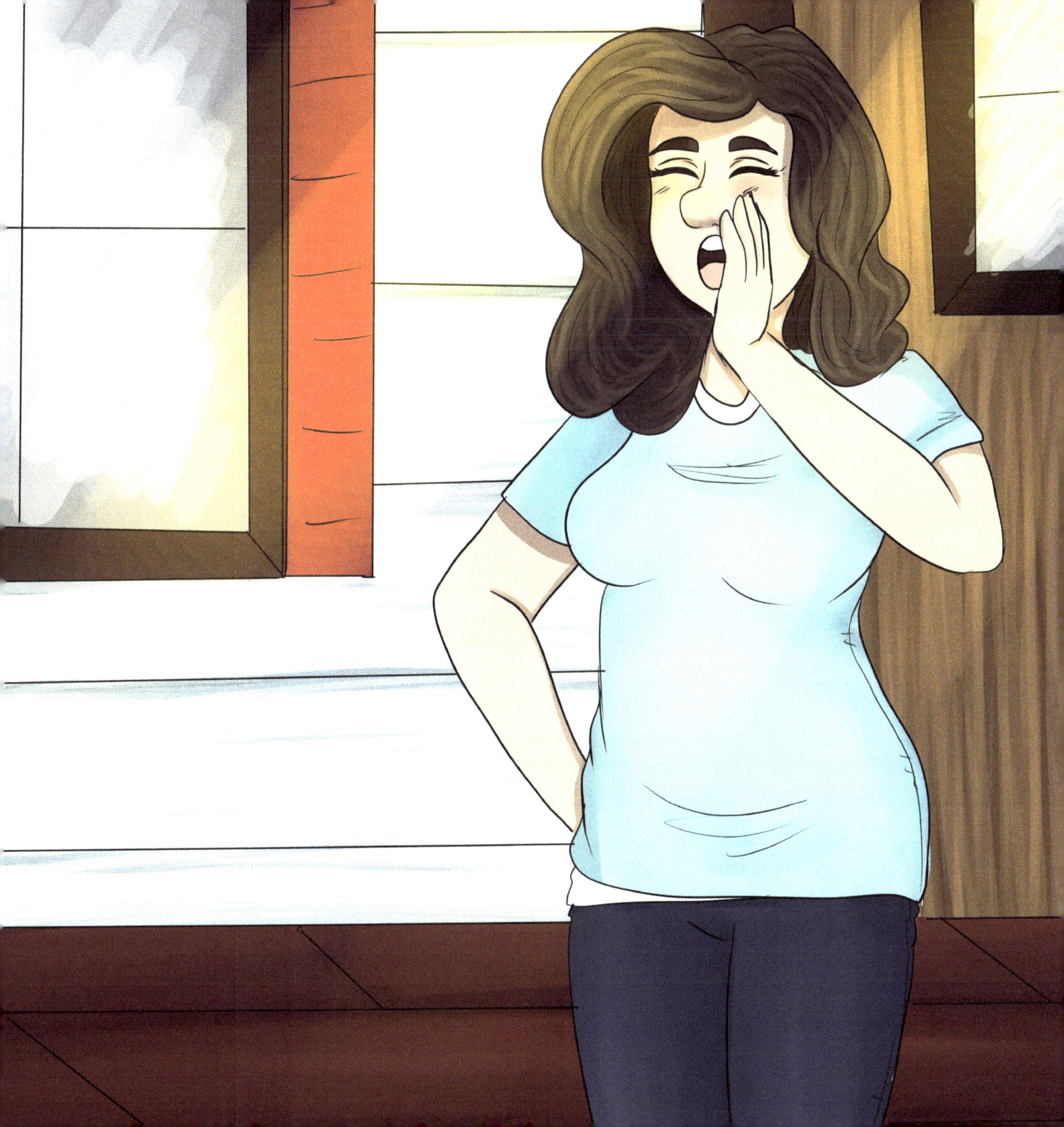

Later grandma began telling the boys of their daily chores which included watering the gardens. She told them that in the middle of the day, they were free to do what they wanted.

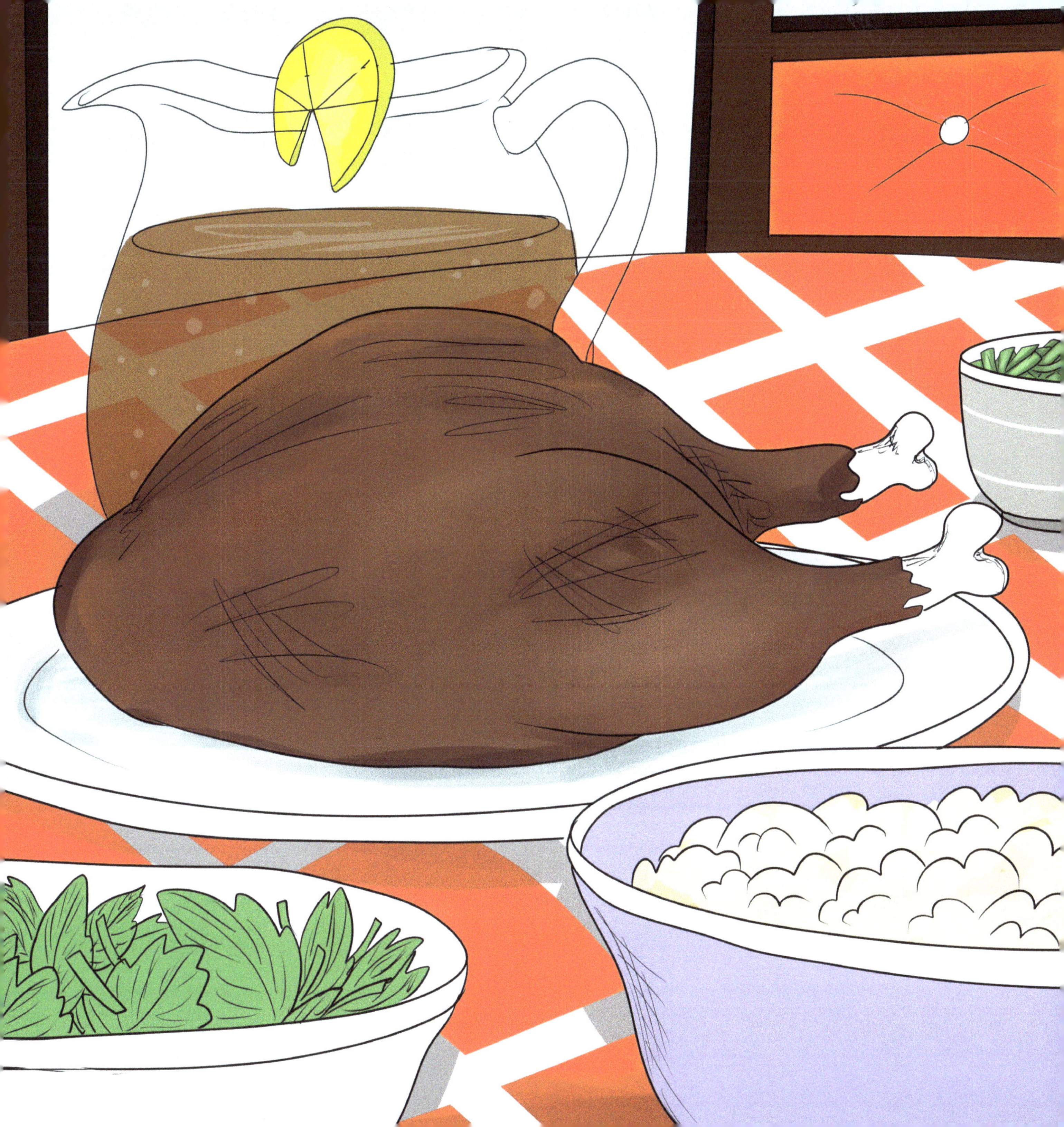

The weekend went by fast; it was Sunday evening. Mom and Dad were getting ready to leave. They hugged the boys and told them to be good and off they went.

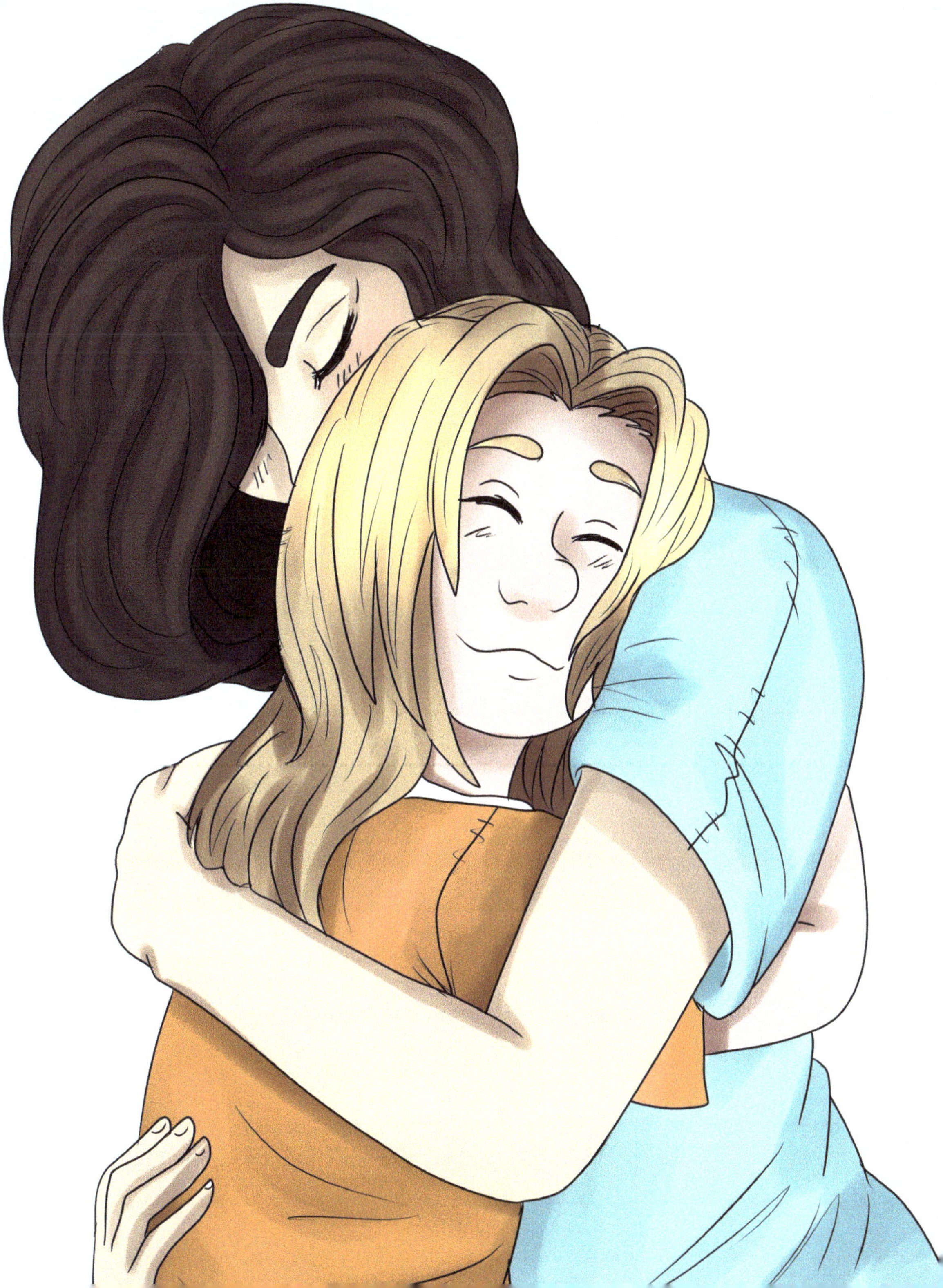

That night they lay in their bed dreaming of going fishing and riding the horses. They couldn't wait!

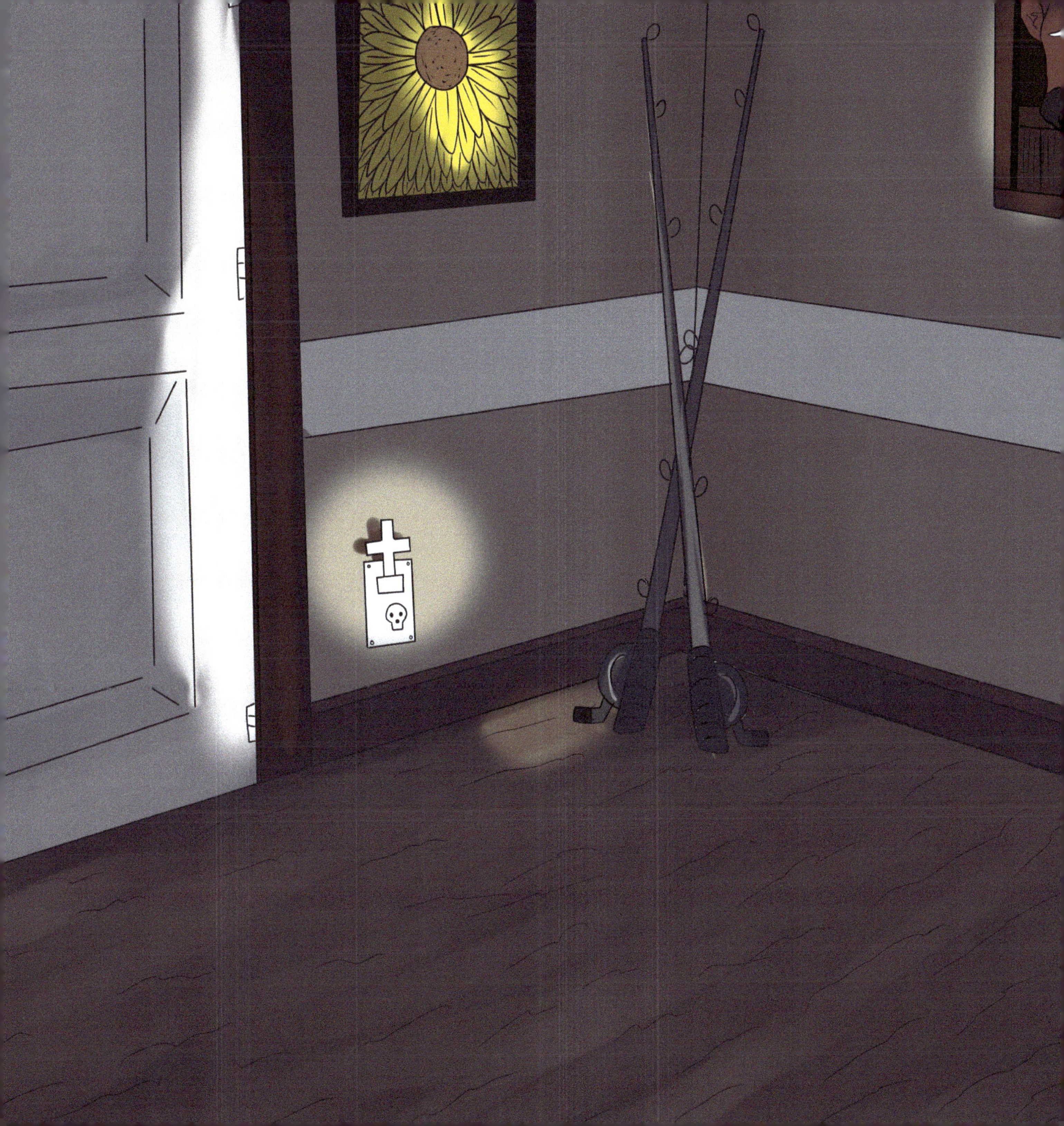

Grandma was up really early; that was something the boys were not expecting. It was still dark outside when grandma came into their room.

"Rise and shine! It is five o'clock! Time to get up, greet the day, eat and feed the animals!"

They rolled over, stretched, let out a big yawn and said, "Oh grandma, can't we sleep a little bit longer?"

"Nope," grandma said, "The animals are hungry and if you want to go fishing, you have to feed the animals first."

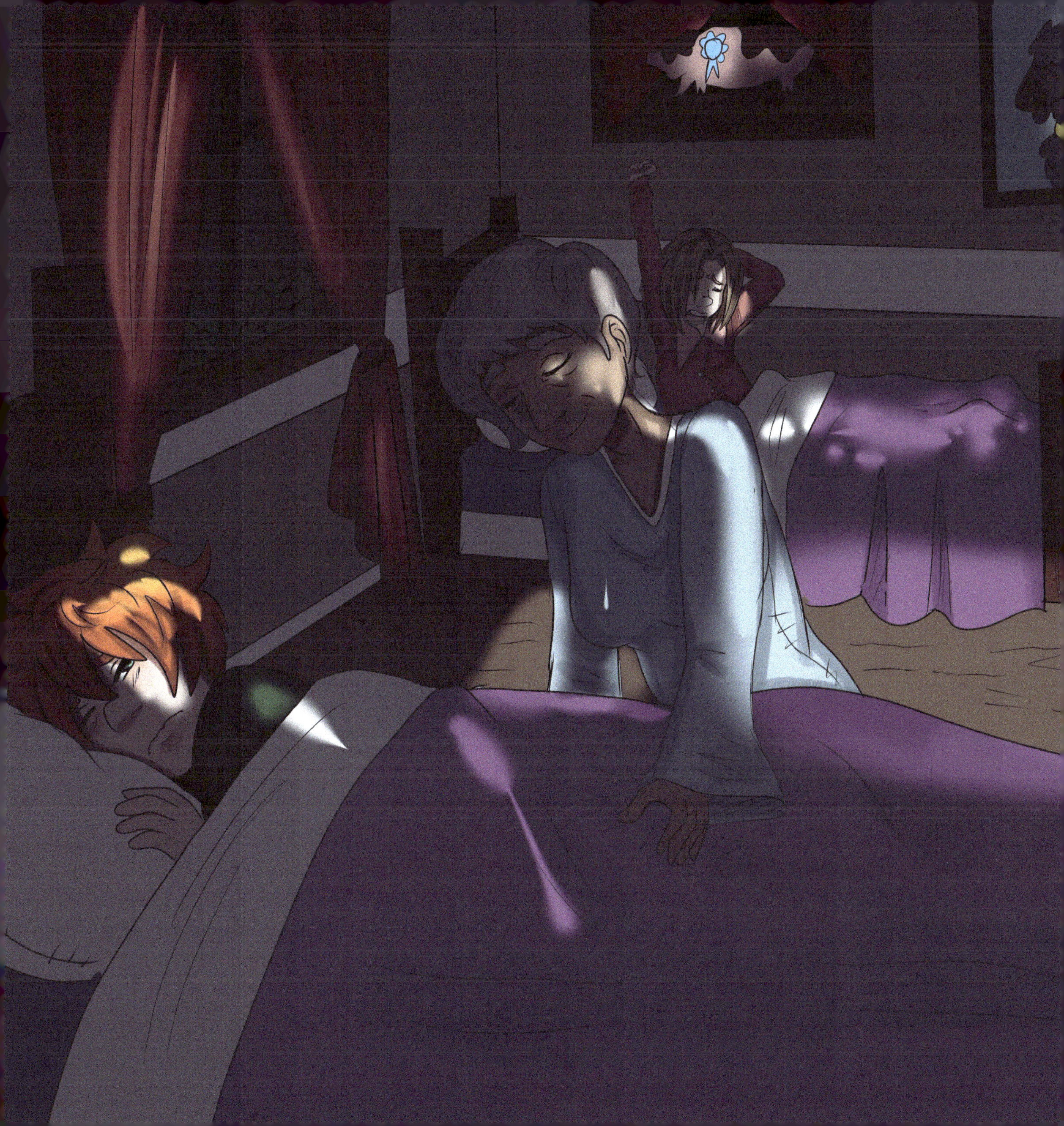

Finally dressed, they ran into the kitchen, "That smells good! What are you fixing grandma?"

"Bacon and pancakes, do you have big appetites?" Grandma asked.

"We sure do, especially for bacon!" They replied.

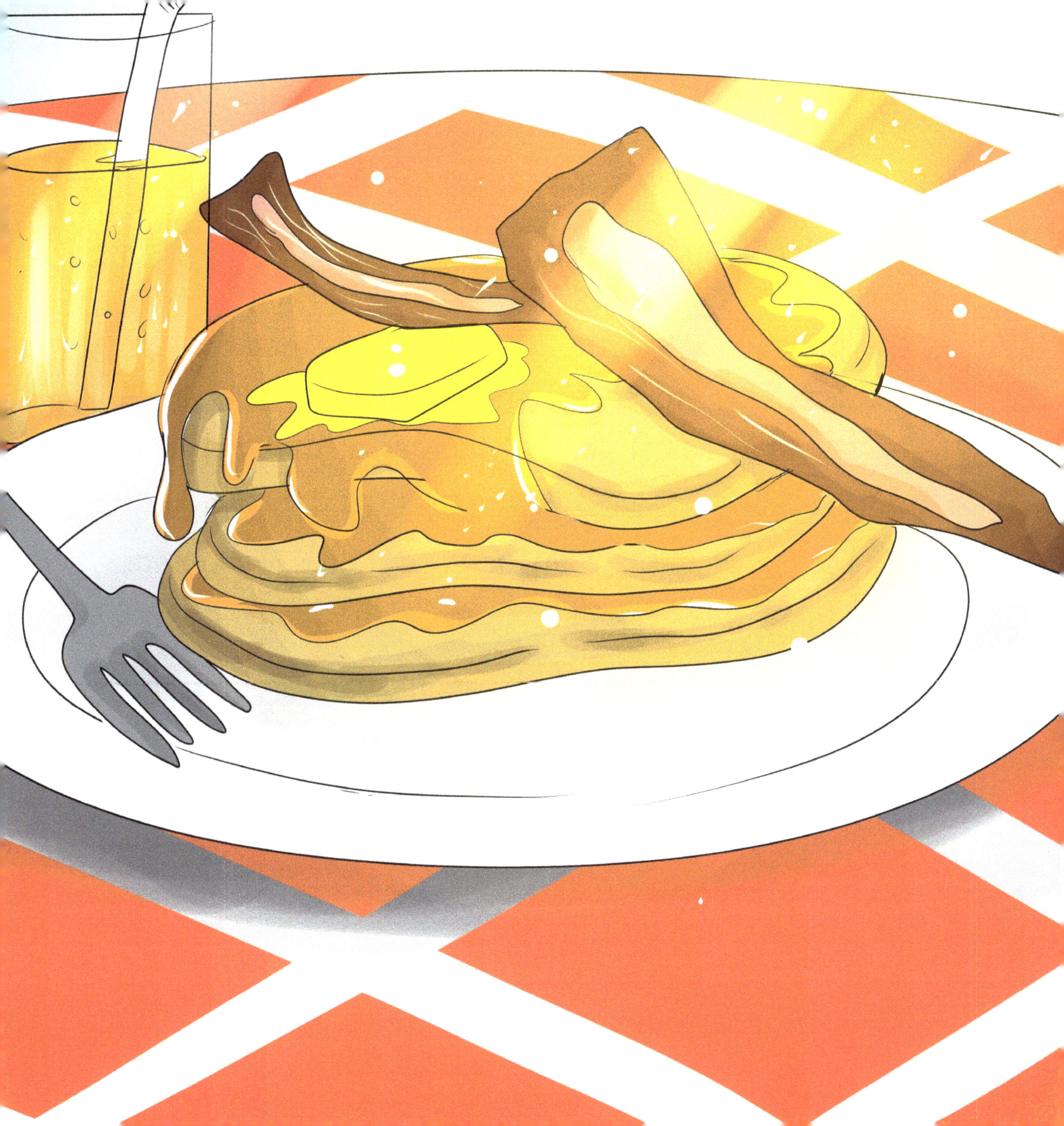

Excited about finishing their chores and heading for the pond, they got the baskets and headed for the chickens coop to collect the eggs first. That was a mistake! A rooster came flying out of the coop and started chasing Timmy all the way around the pen!

"Grandma, Grandma, help, help!" Gerald Ray shouted.

"Grandma, a rooster is chasing Timmy! Help!"

Timmy screamed for help as he ran around the chicken coop not knowing what to do!

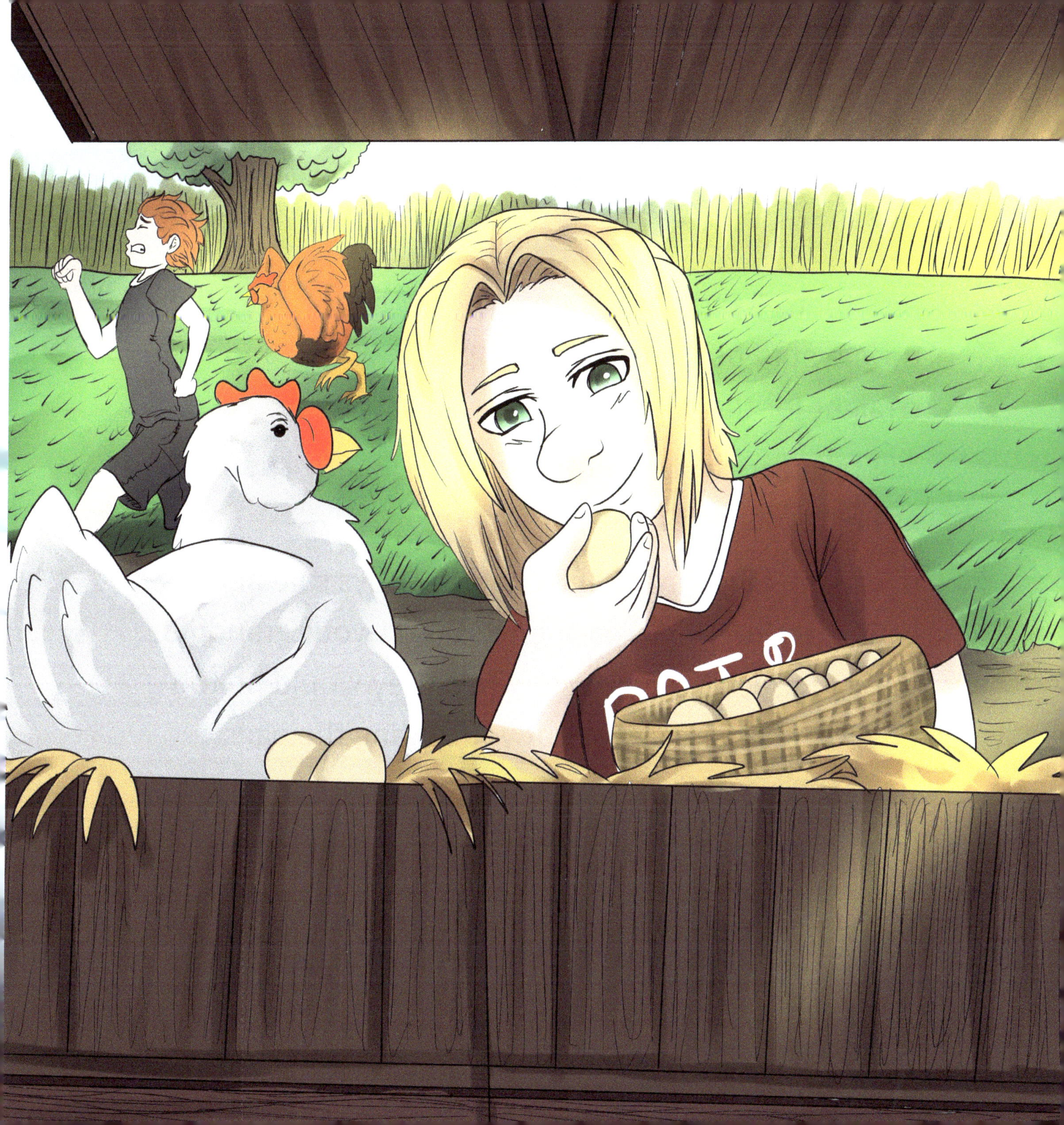

Just then, Randy drove up. He was aware that the boys would be there for a couple of weeks and ran straight for the coop.

"I'll take care of them Mrs. Lewis!" Randy shouted, as he headed for Timmy.

It wasn't long until Randy had the boys safe and sound again. He asked them, "Didn't your grandma tell you to feed them first? Then they would be too busy eating to worry about you getting the eggs from their nest."

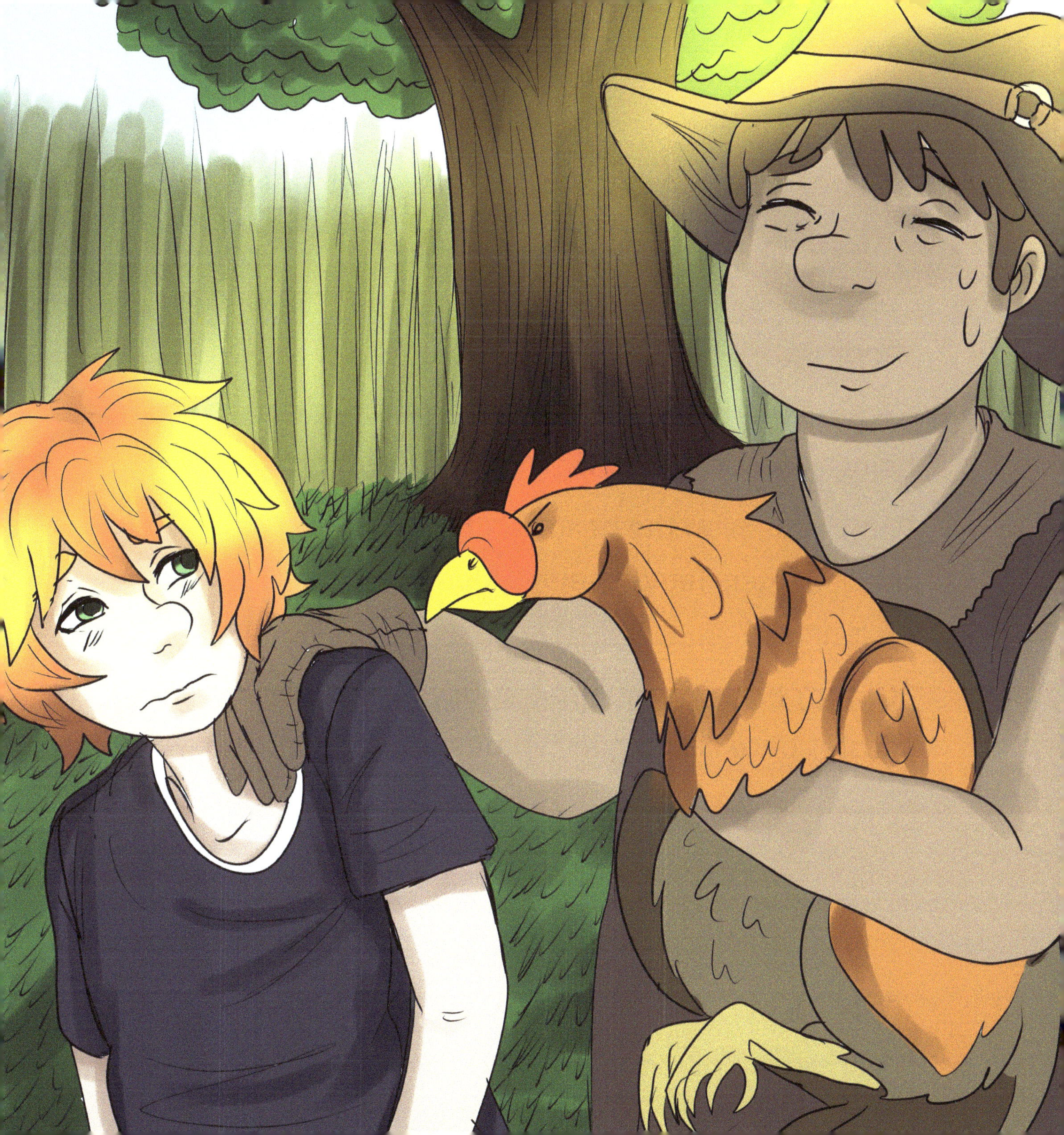

"Yes, she told us," Timmy said still looking kind of shook up.

Gerald Ray piped in, "But we got excited about being almost finished with chores and forgot."

Patting them on the head and trying to hold back the laughter, Randy said, "I bet you won't forget next time?"

"Oh no, I don't want that again. Being chased by a rooster once is enough!" Timmy shouted.

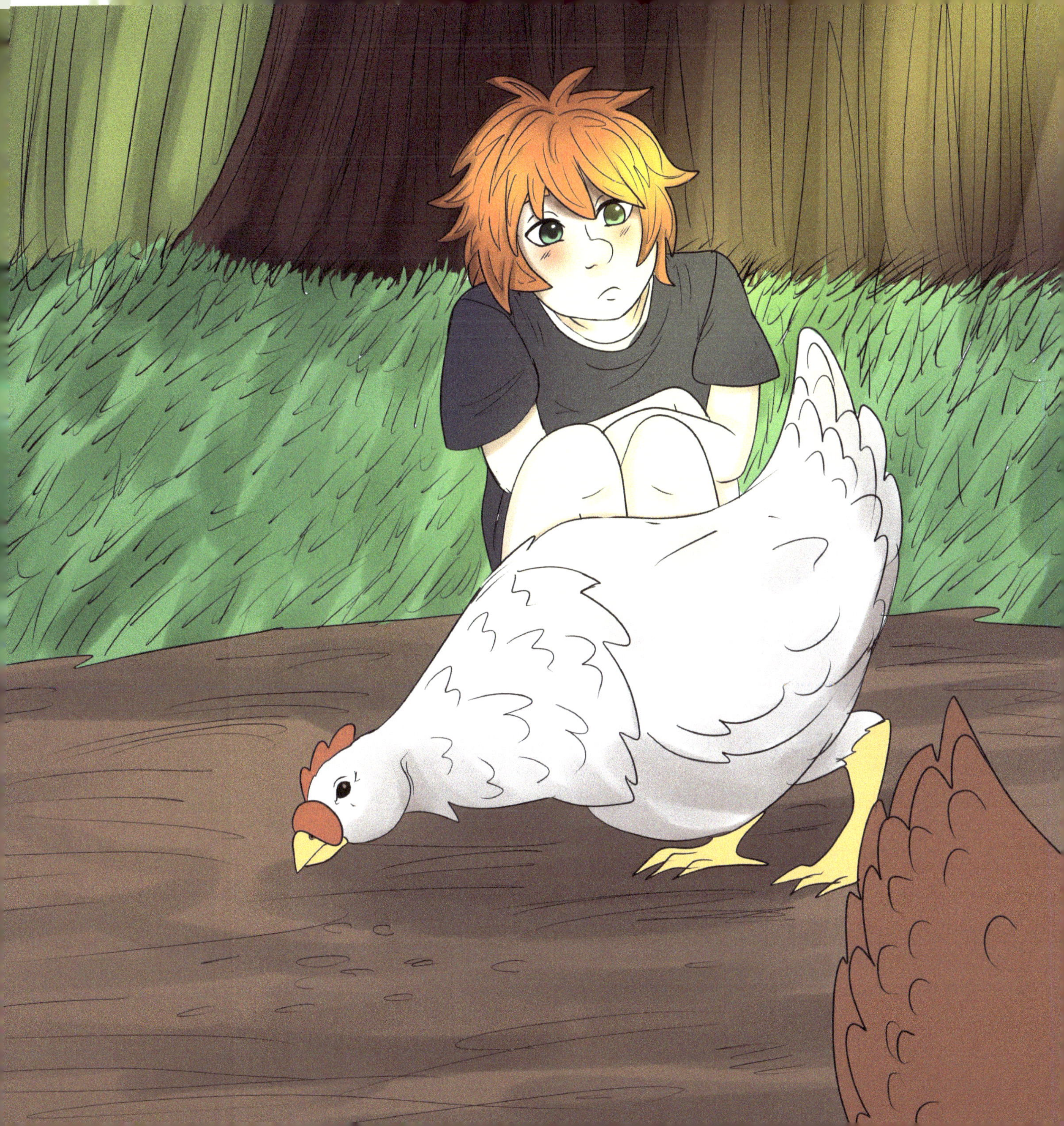

"Well, I guess you met the boys," grandma said as she came down from the porch.

The rest of the day, the boys followed Randy around and he showed them the animals and told them their names. The horses were both male, the brown horse was Madison and the white and brown spotted one was Patchwork.

Randy let the boys pet them. He said, "Gently stroke them so they know they can trust you. Let them get to know you and after a couple of days I will help you to ride them."

"Ok," the boys replied.

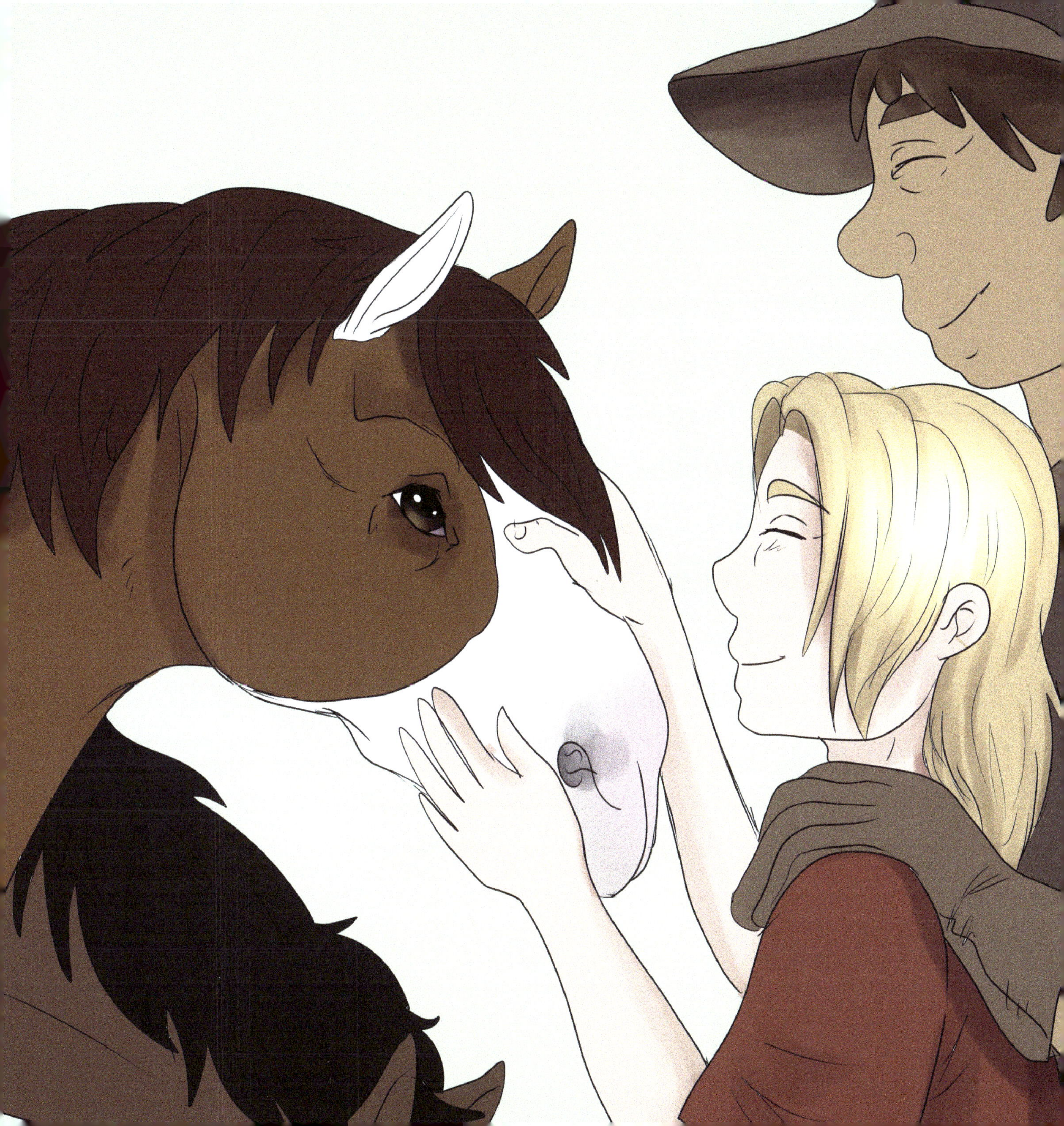

Chores done; it was time to go fishing!

They ran inside, grabbed their lunch and bottled water and headed to the barn where Dad had put their fishing poles.

Grandma was weeding in her garden. They yelled good-bye and said they would be back in a couple of hours.

"Have a good time and be careful!"

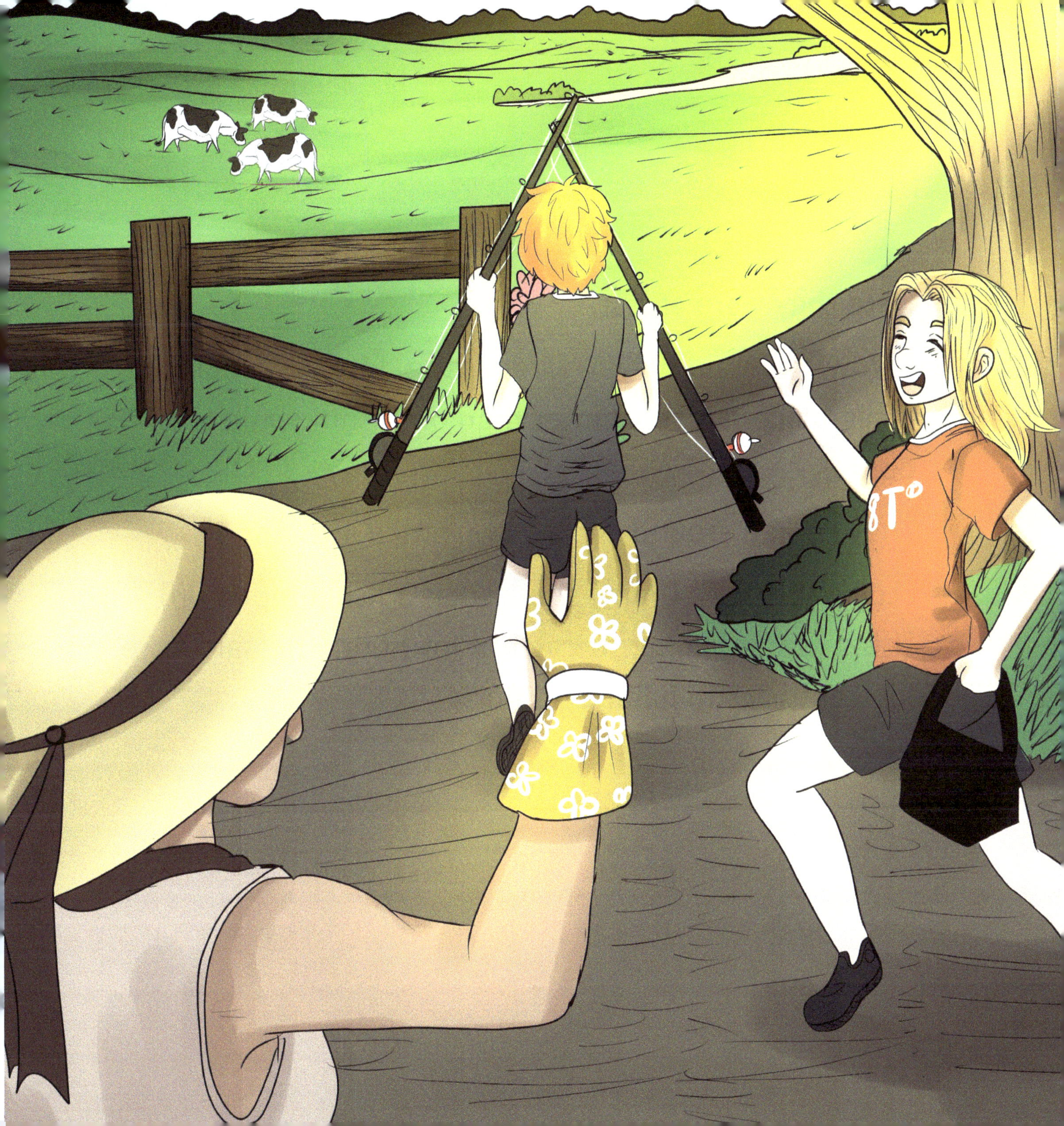

Here they were at last!

"Wow!" Gerald Ray yelled as he looked around. "This place is even better than our fishing hole at home!

They looked around and finally settled into a spot.

"Look at that!" Timmy shouted as a fish jumped up! "I bet we are going to catch a lot here," he said as he went back to baiting his hook.

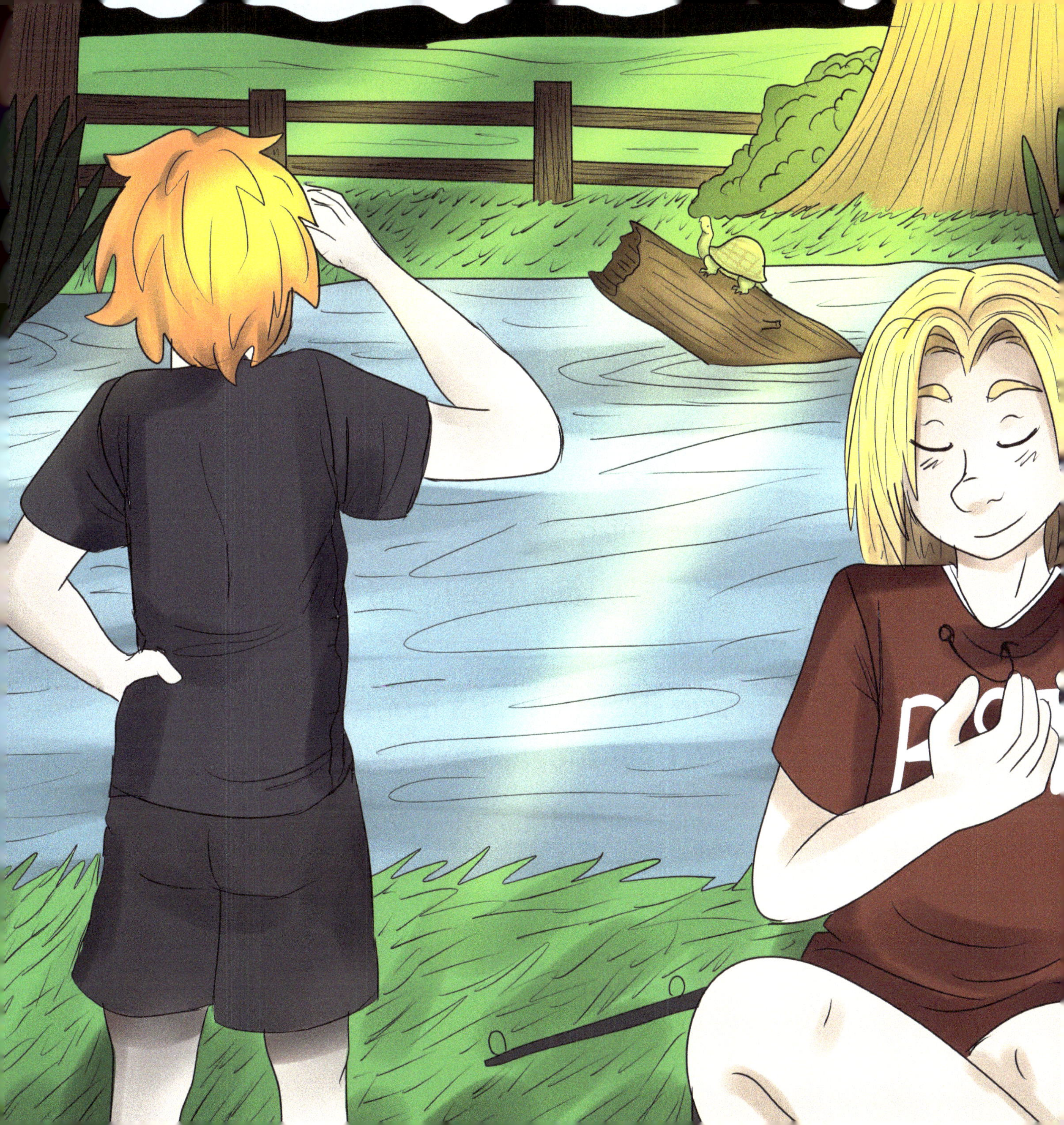

They caught eight fish! Their stomachs were growling. They looked at each other and Timmy said, "It must be lunch time; let's go eat."

"I agree! I'm starving," Gerald Ray replied.

"I think this is going to be a great summer after all; even if we have to do chores. I like it out here," Timmy said as he finished up.

Agreeing, Gerald Ray said, "Yeah and I can't wait to ride the horses!"

They got up and stretched for a moment, "Me too," Timmy said and then added, "It's hot isn't it?"

Wiping the sweat off of his forehead Gerald Ray said, "Yeah it sure is!"

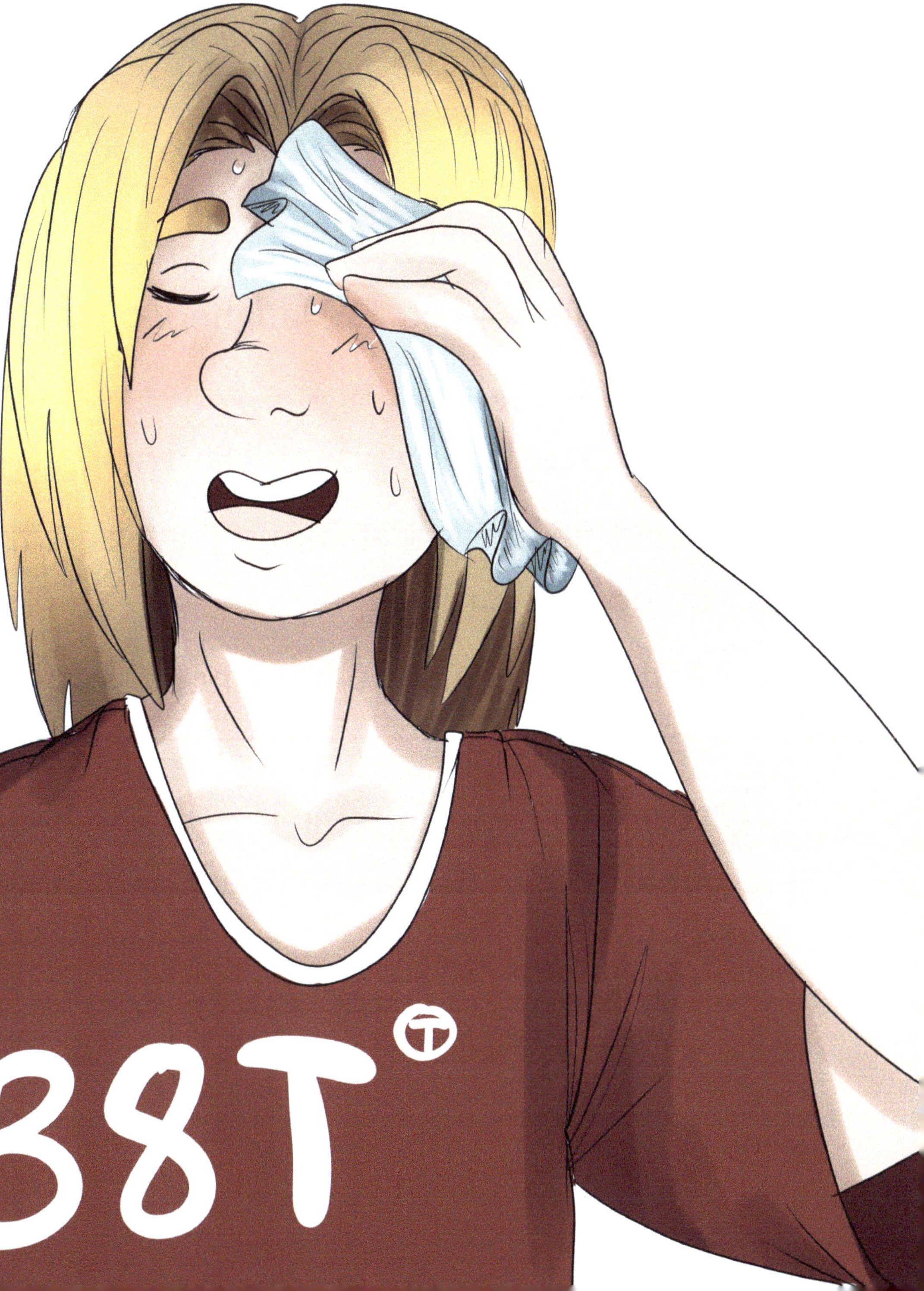
B8T

Timmy yelled back, "Hey, I can help with that!" Then he reached over and pushed Gerald Ray in the pond! He laughed and laughed!

Gerald Ray got out of the water with an angry look on his face. Timmy was still laughing.

Gerald Ray yelled at him, "That isn't fair, what did you do that for?"

Timmy shouted, "You were hot, I was just helping to cool you off!"

"Well," Gerald Ray replied, "Let me help you do the same!" Then he reached over and shoved Timmy in the water.

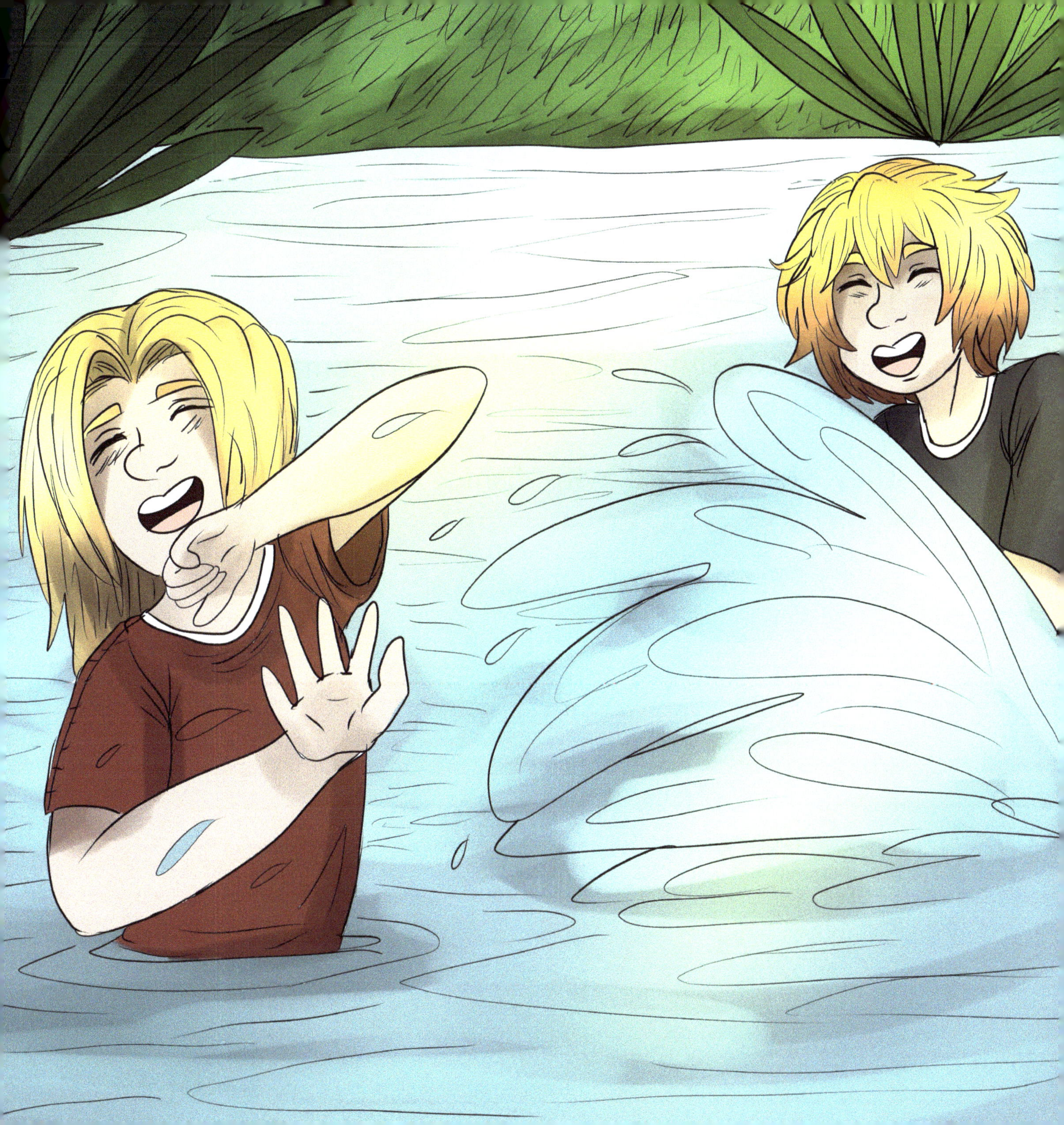

They laughed and laughed.

Getting out Timmy said, "I hope grandma won't be mad."

They started back with fishing poles and fish in hand, soaking wet!

Grandma was sitting on the porch as they walked up, "What did you do?"

"We kind of fell in," Timmy said.

"That isn't true," Gerald Ray said, "You pushed me in so I pushed you back."

"Well," grandma started in, "Go in and get dried off."

"You mean you're not mad?" They asked.

"Of course not, it is summer and hot and that is what the pond is there for!"

They were amazed at her answer. As they were playing with scruffy, grandma shouted out the door for them to start watering the garden and the flowers.

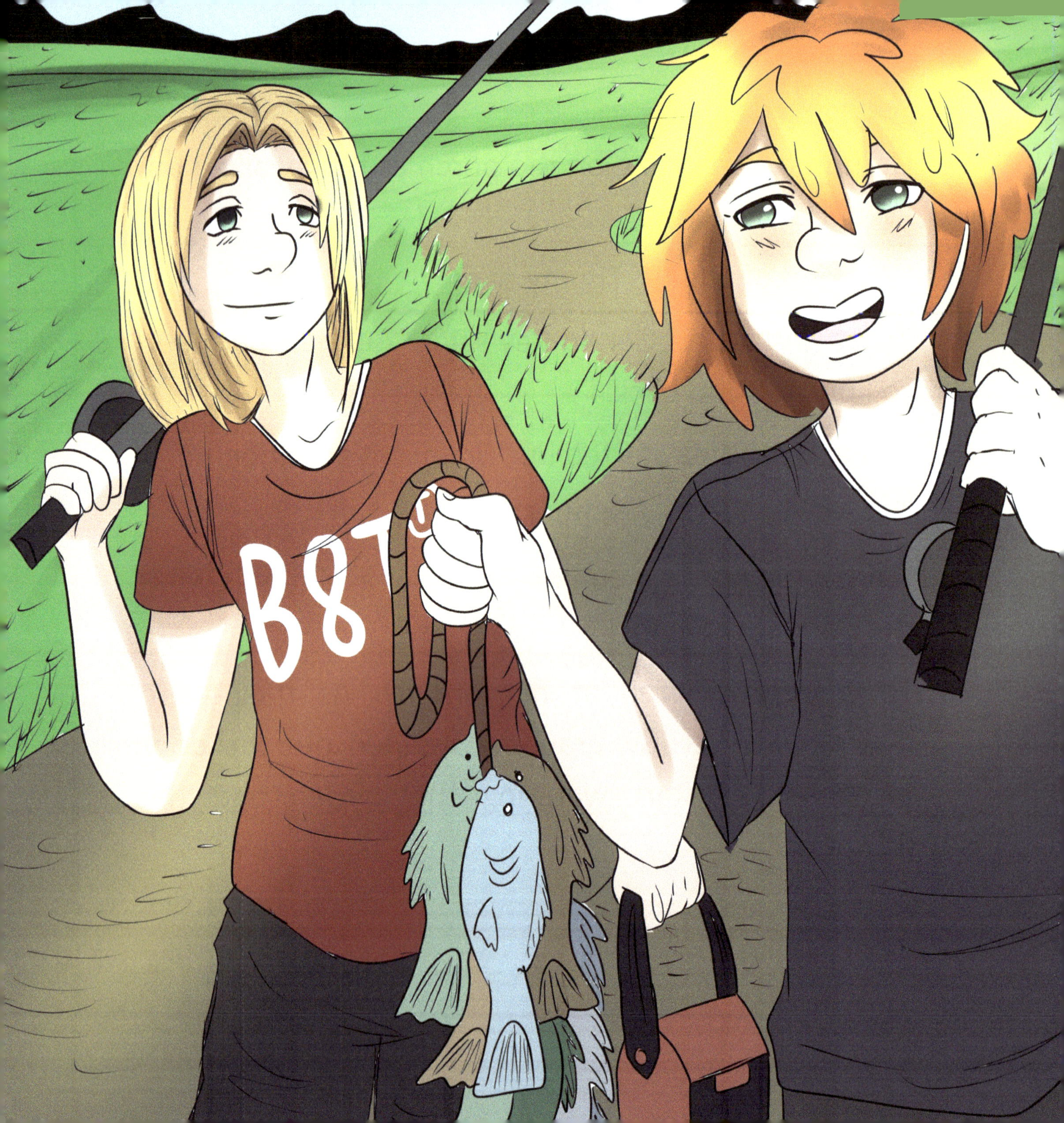
B8T

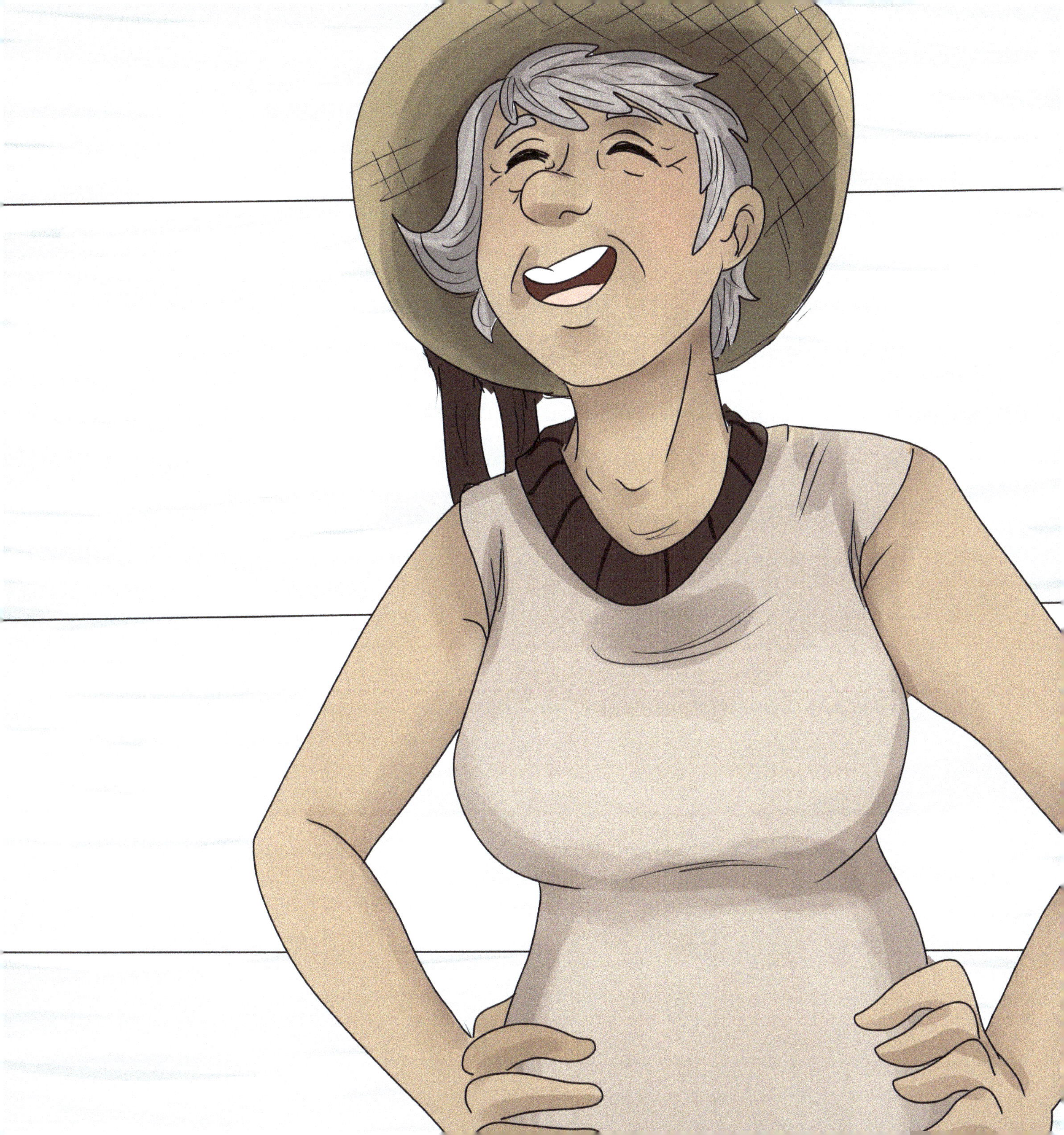

Time was going by fast, they even learned to ride the horses! They loved that! The boys learned a lot about animals, how a farm works, and how useful farms were to everyone; even the big ones with huge crops that sell to grocery stores. They were having a great time.

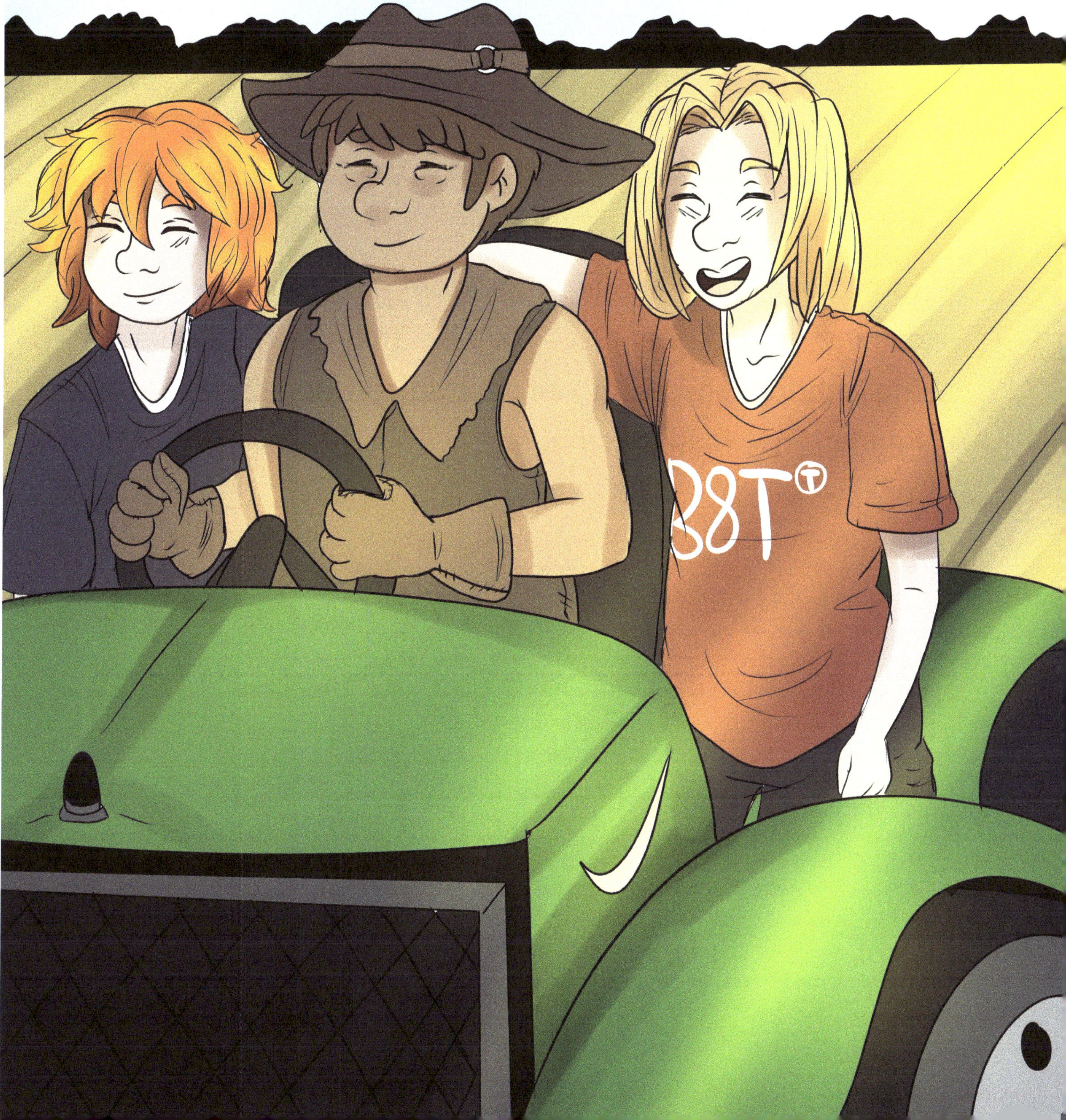
38T

Tomorrow was Sunday, and Mom and Dad were coming to get them after church. They finished up their chores and went out to ride the horses with Randy. They really liked him.

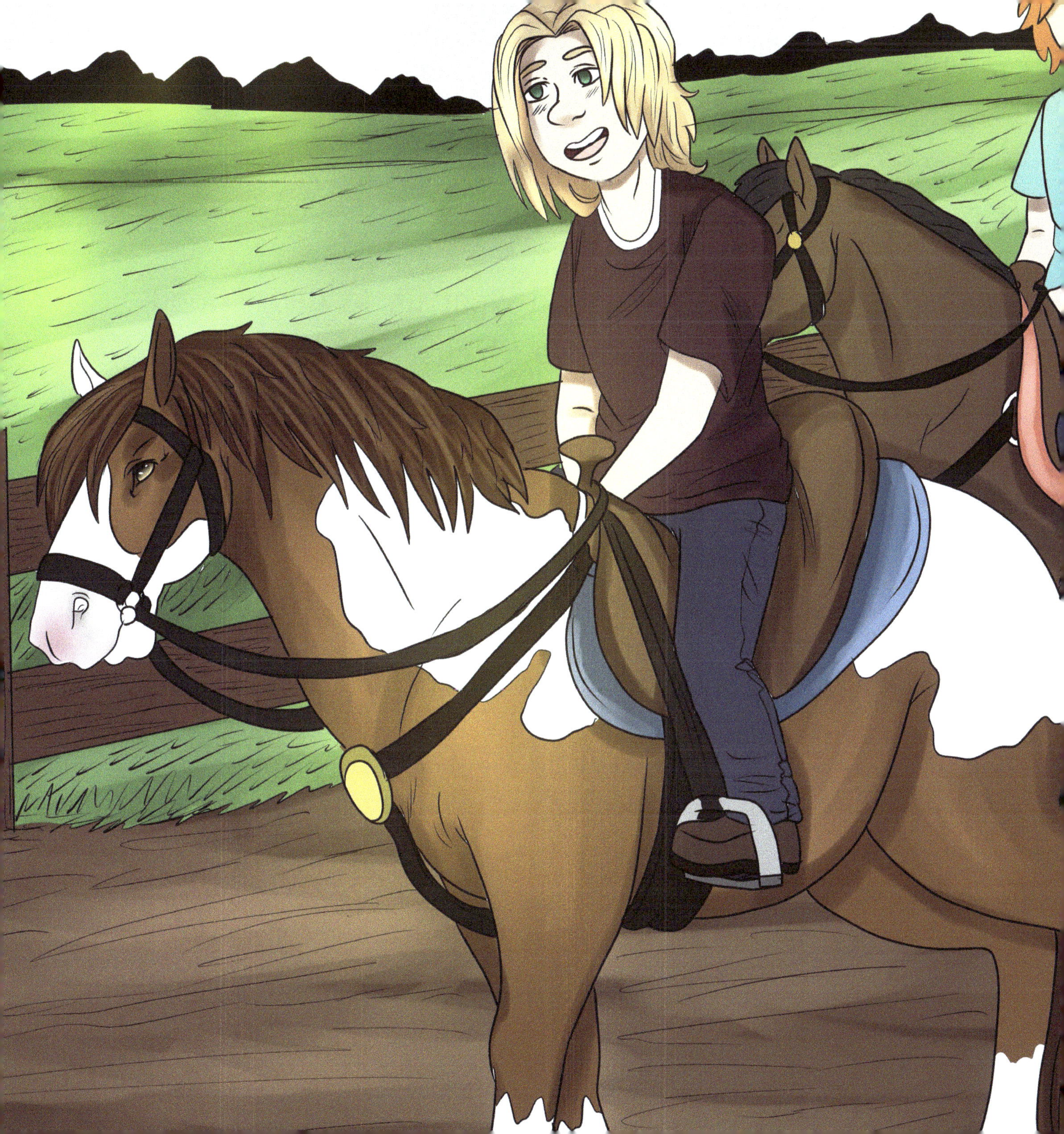

They had a long day and went up to bed, "Good night grandma, we love you."

Tucking them into bed she smiled and said, "Good night, I love you too. I have had so much fun with you boys. I will miss you when you leave. You have been a real big help to me."

They said together, "We liked helping and had more fun even doing the chores than we thought we would."

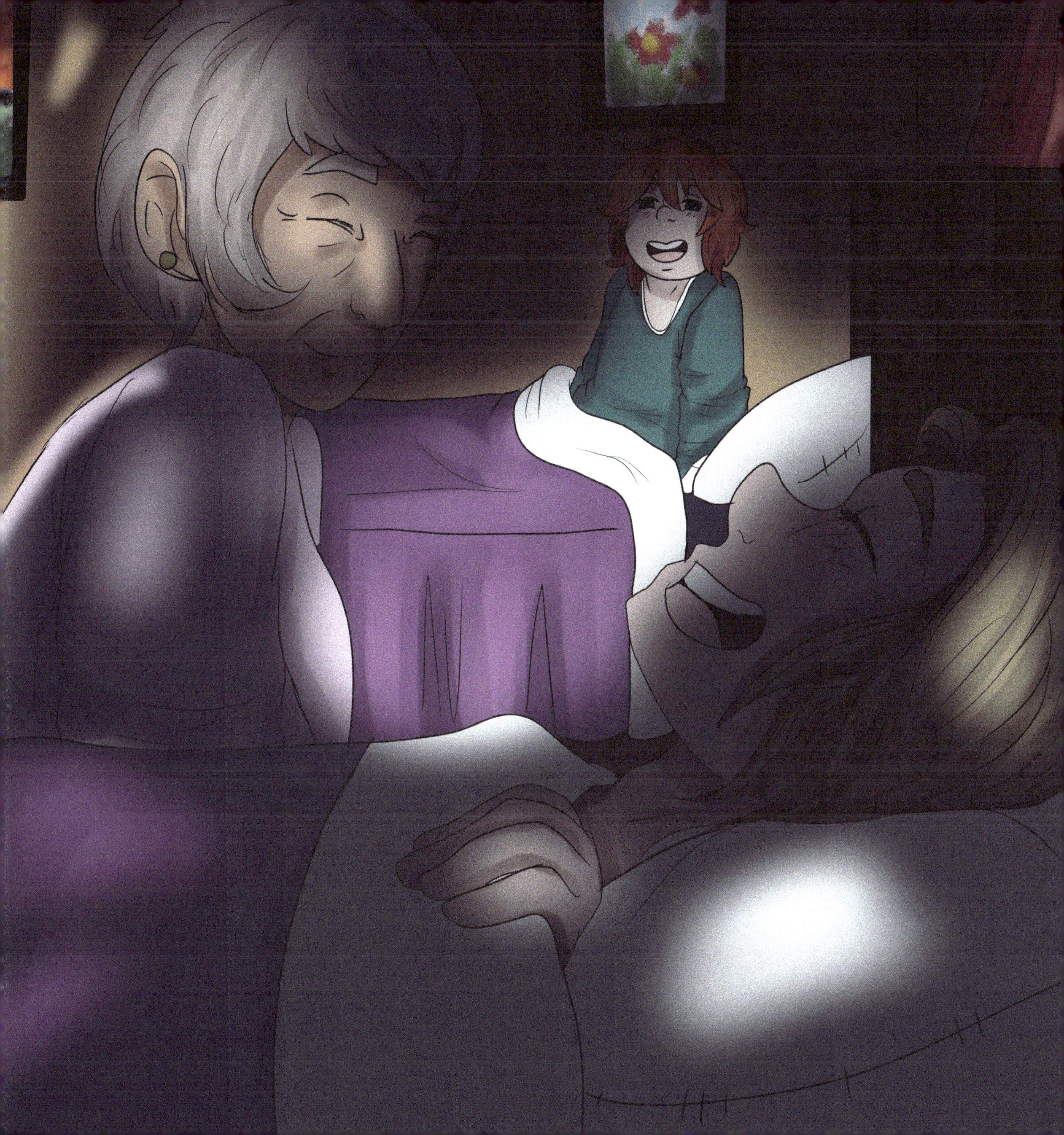

It was Sunday, they were going to grandma's church, which was kind of small. It was white and had a big steeple on the top of the roof. Her pastor was real nice. He preached about the Trinity: Three in One: God the Father, the Son and the Holy Spirit. This puzzled Gerald Ray. He couldn't quite understand how that could be. He couldn't get it out of his mind.

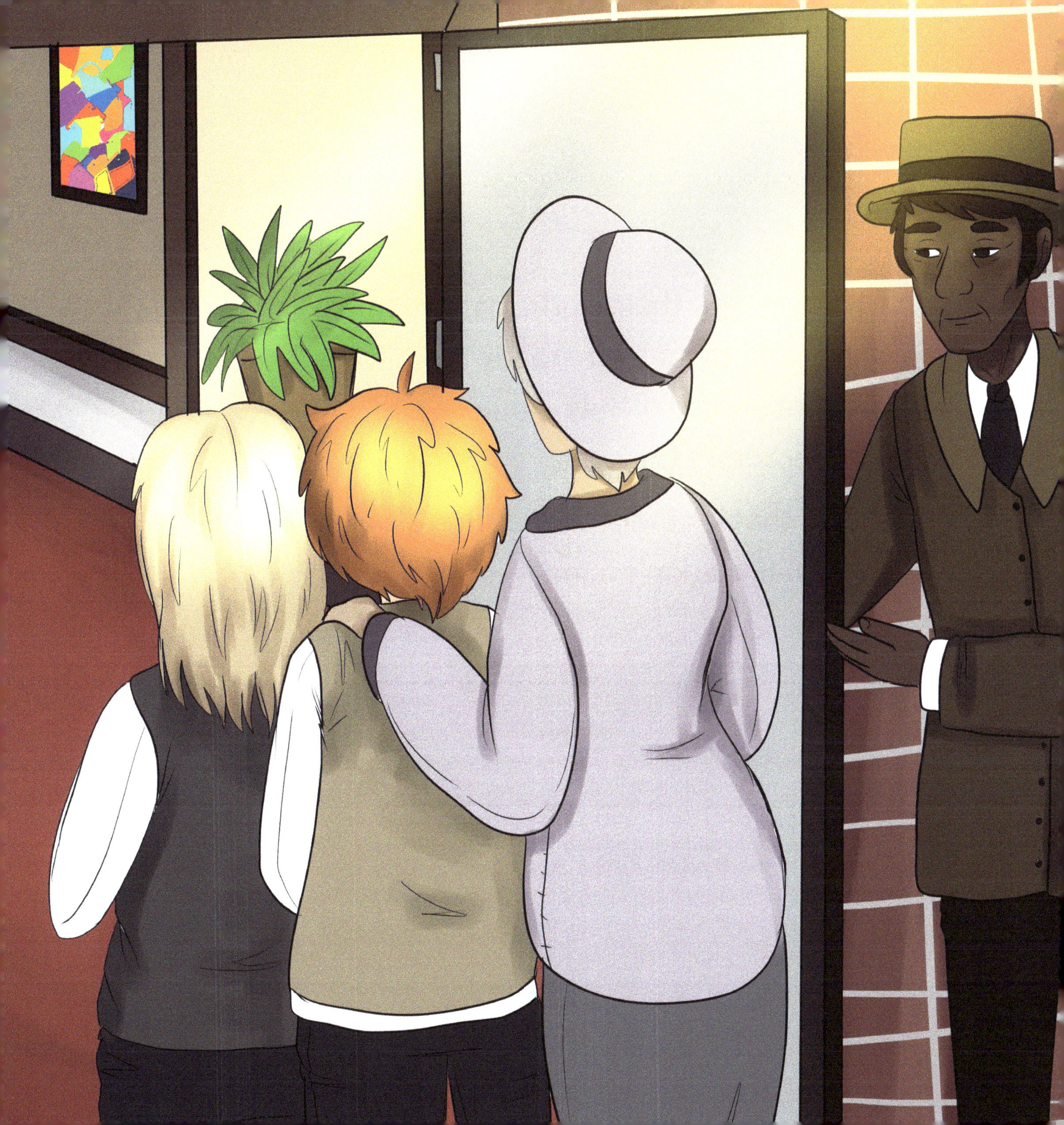

They changed their clothes after church and packed their things to get ready for Mom and Dad. Grandma asked if they would water the garden and flowers before they left.

They shook their head in agreement, "Sure grandma, we don't mind."

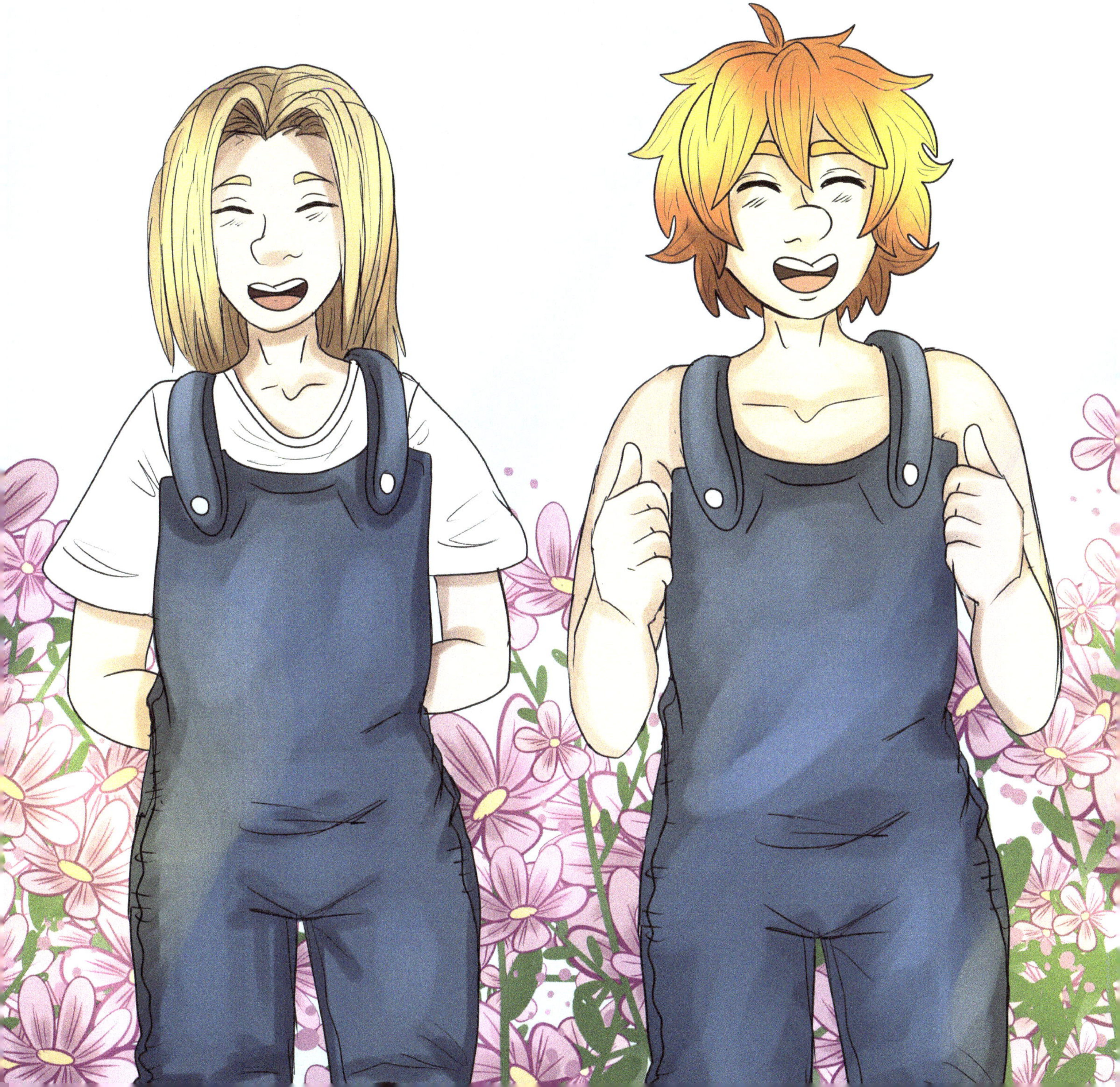

Right then they heard a car and Gerald Ray ran over to the window, "Its Mom and Dad!"

They ran out to meet them and began telling them all that they had done before they hardly had time enough to get out of the car.

"So, I guess it wasn't so bad," Dad said as he walked up to the house.

"We had a great time!" Timmy shouted walking along side of him.

They told them the events of their stay, even the rooster chasing Timmy around the chicken coop. Then they went outside to do their chores one last time before they left.

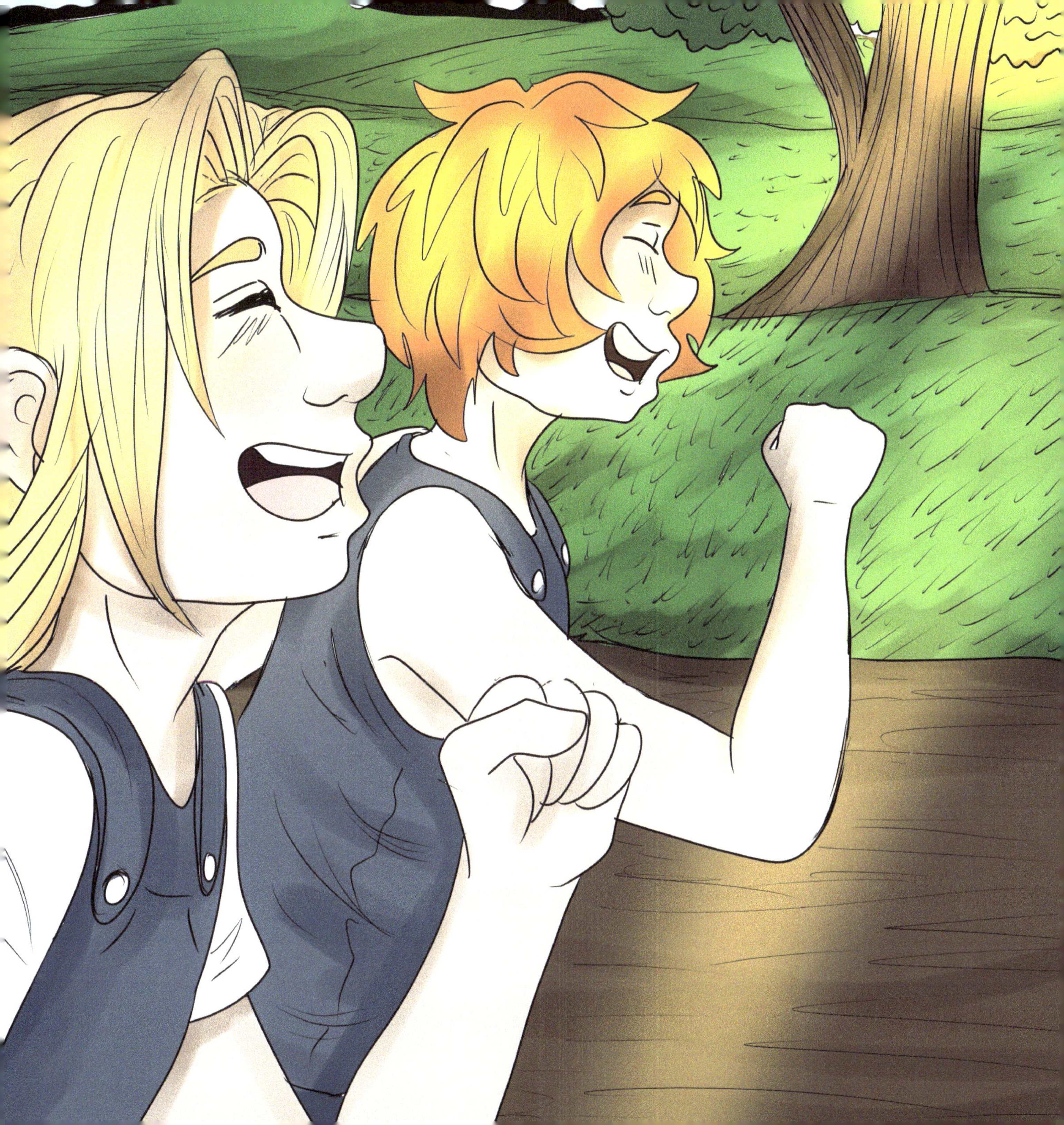

As they began watering grandma's garden Gerald Ray asked Tim, "How can three be in one like the Pastor said? He said God the Father, Jesus Christ the Son, and the Holy Spirit are one yet three separate. How can that be?"

Tim, studied the question in his mind for a while. Finishing up in the vegetable garden they moved on to the flowers. Tim still had not responded.

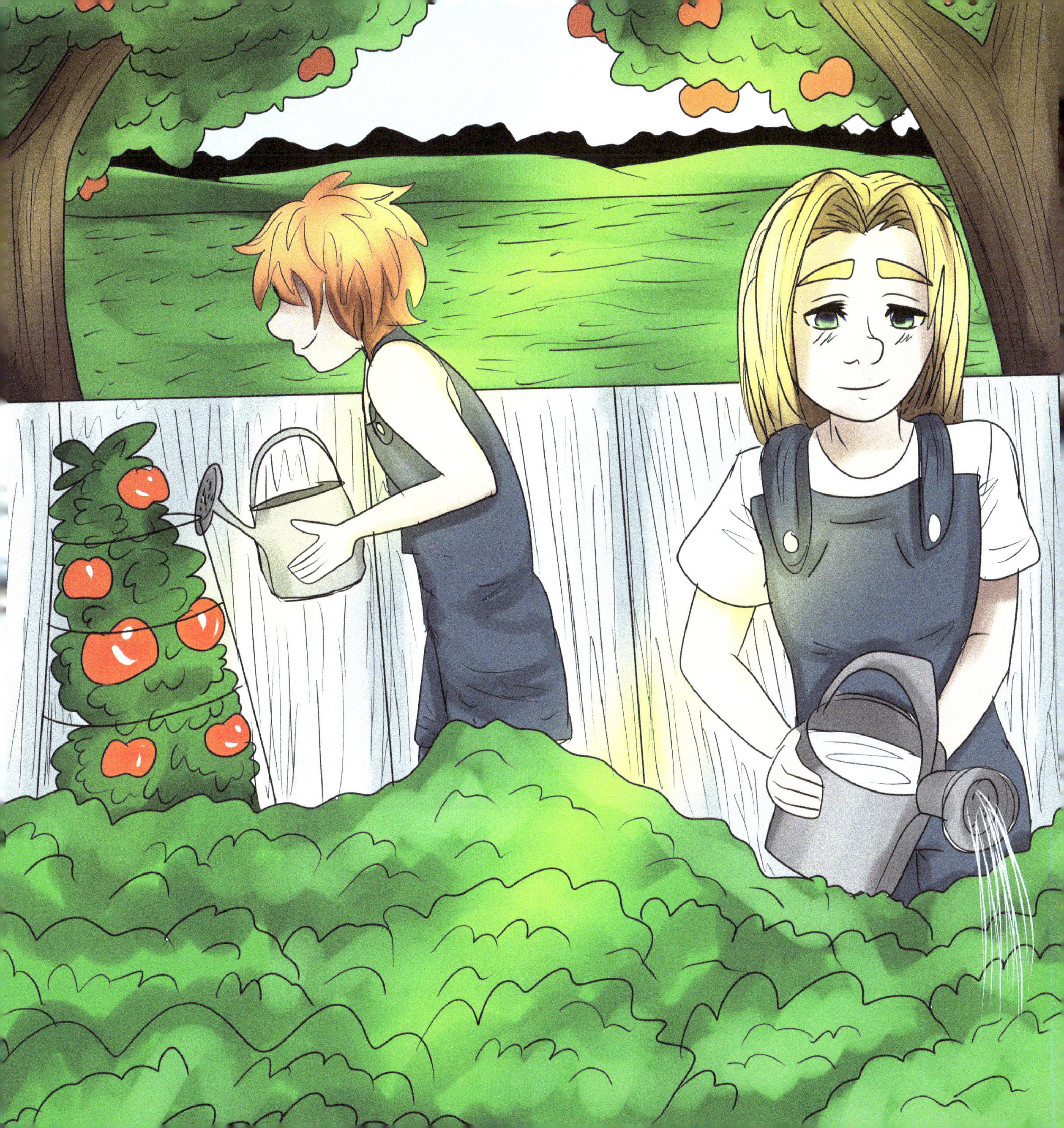

As they moved on from the garden to watering grandma's flowers, Timmy saw a gold pot on the porch with three beautiful purple flowers. Right then, he gets it! He remembered studying colors in Sunday school at home. The gold color he remembers symbolized God and His authority as God and His deity. The purple symbolized the royalty of Jesus Christ.

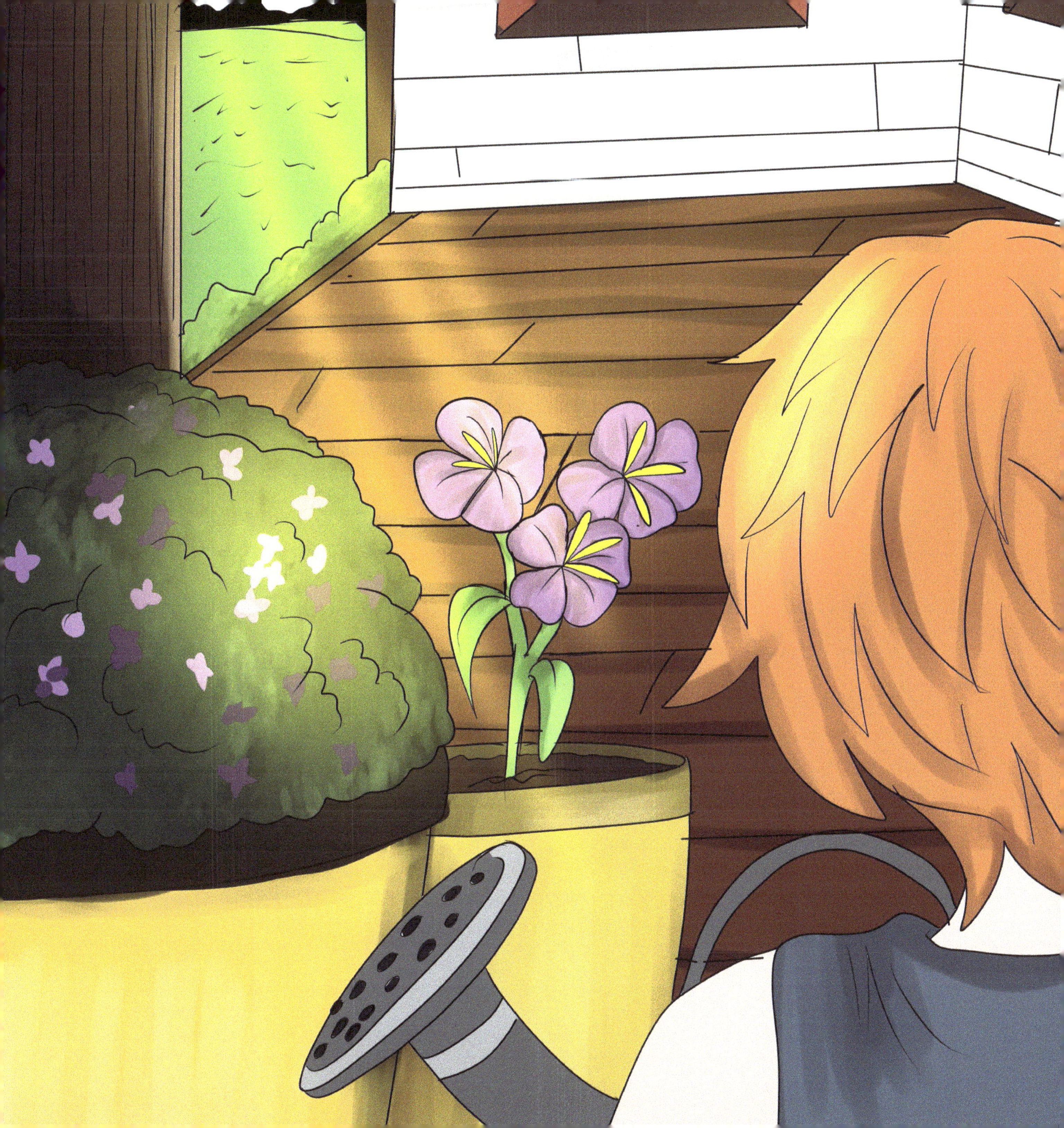

"I got it! I got it!" He shouted! "Look at the gold flower pot on grandma's porch; gold represents God and it has three purple flowers in it. Well all three flowers are in the same pot, one plant but three separate flowers. That is the way it is with the Trinity. All come from the same God and out of God you get God the Father, God the Son, Jesus Christ and God the Holy Spirit. Three separate yet in One God."

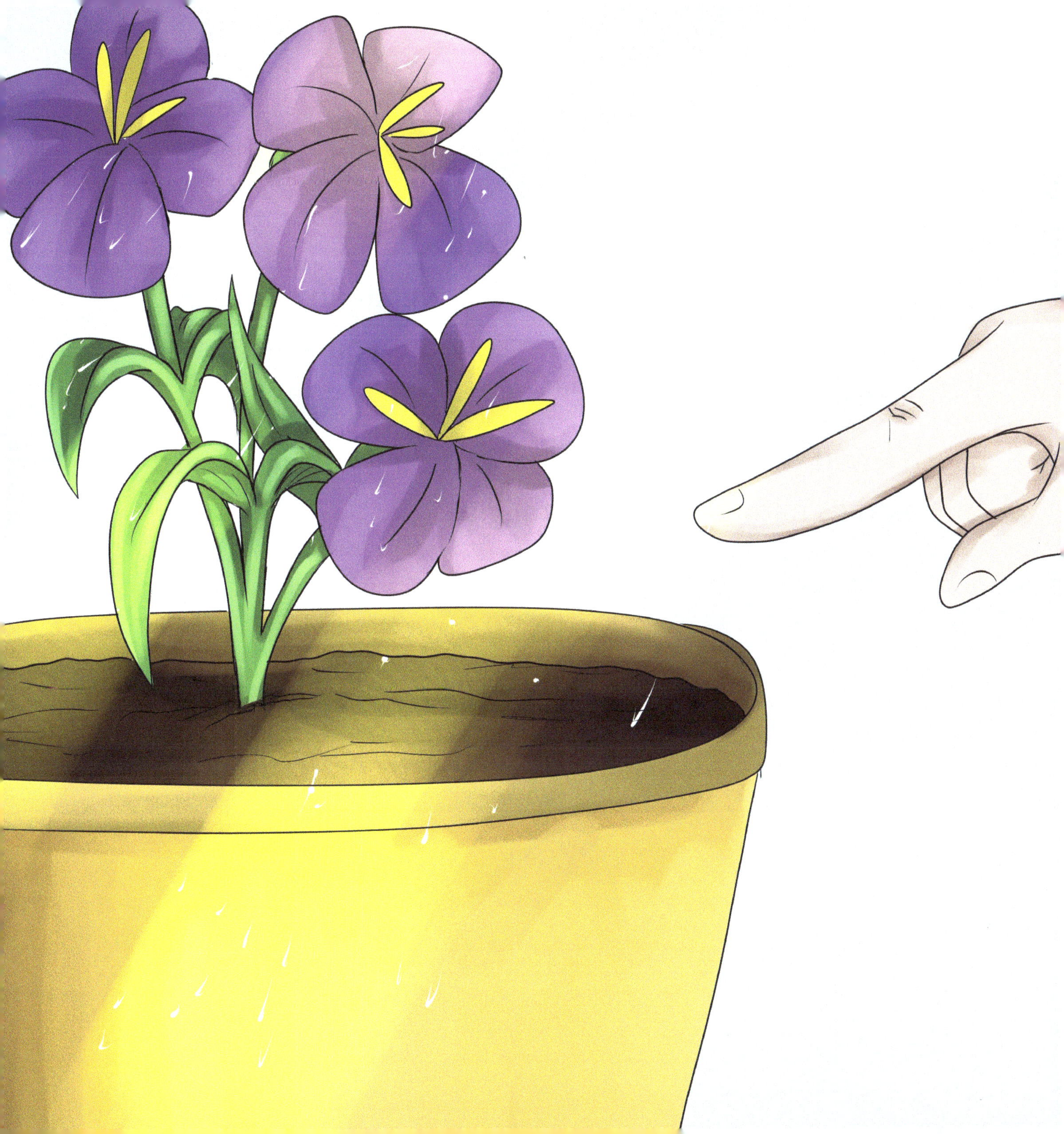

"Wow! Tim, that is great! I understand now! You make it sound so simple. How did you ever get so smart?"

Gerald Ray continued his watering. "Oh, it just comes natural," he said smugly.

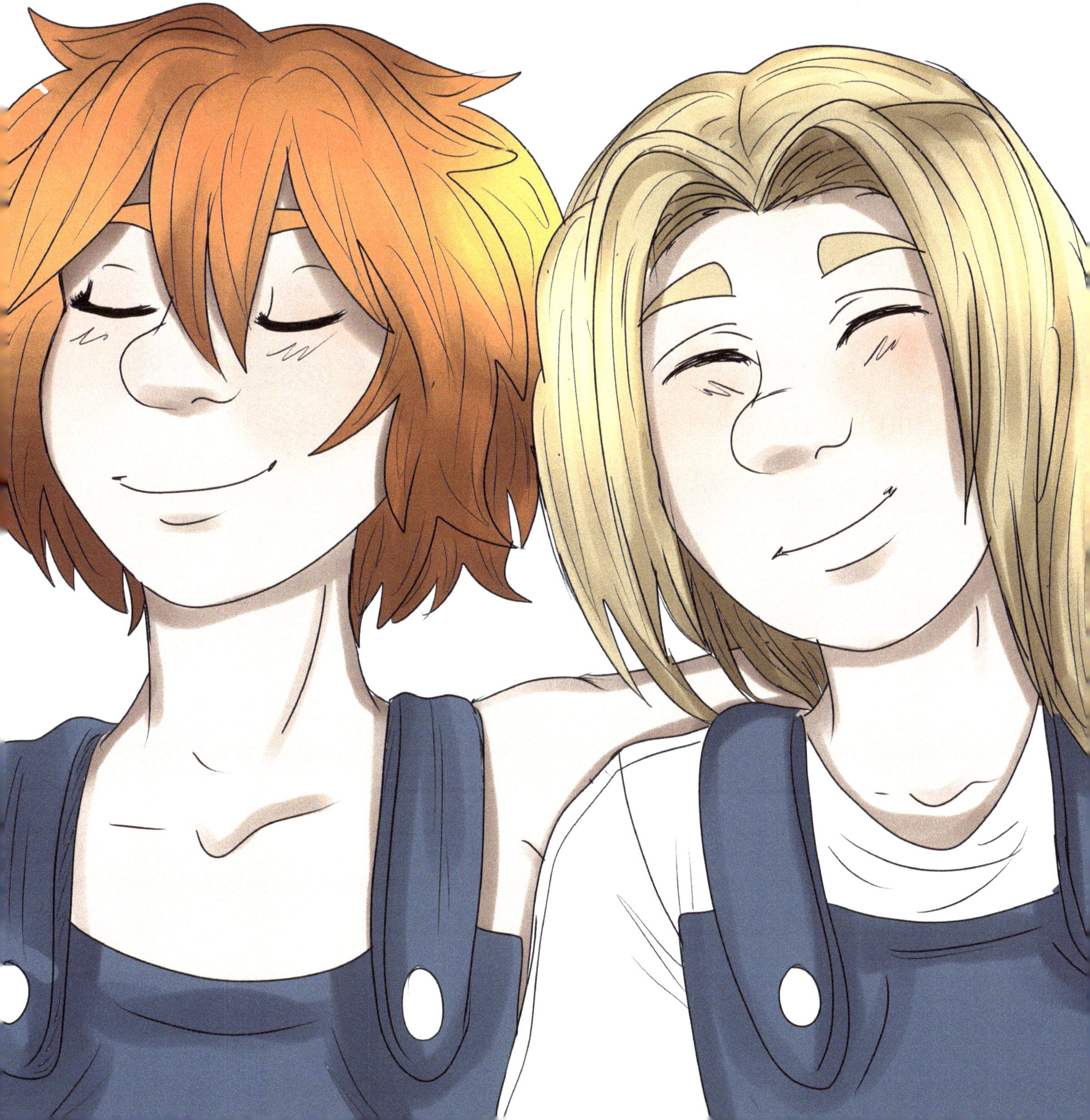

They went back to watering the flowers and Tim looked over at Gerald Ray with a mischievous grin on his face. He slowly turned the water hose toward him and yelled out. He totally drenched him in water! He laughed and laughed!

"Hey! What did you do that for?" Gerald Ray shouted. "I was just baptizing you," Timmy said.

They both burst out laughing. Grandma's farm wasn't that bad after all.

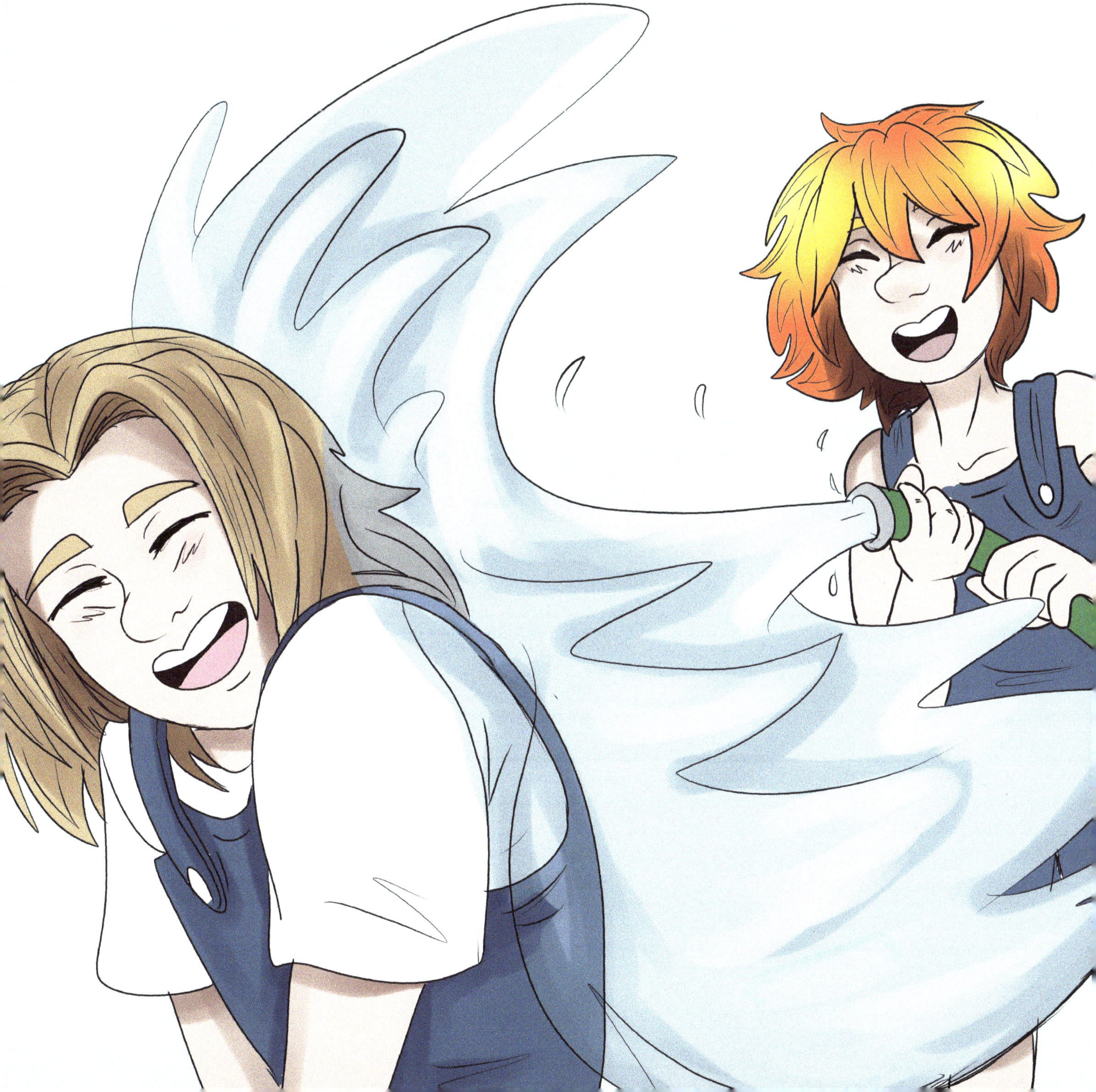

The End

Scripture References

"Go therefore and make disciples of all the nations, baptizing them in the name of the Father and the Son and the Holy Spirit."

                                        Matthew 28:19

Author Sandra (Lott) Smith was born and raised in Texas and is the author of Ride the Wind, God's Love and My Father's Eyes: Seeing Yourself through the Eyes of Love and more. She has learned about the love and faithfulness of God through the death of her sixteen year old son and many other hardships. Through His love and comfort she has drawn close to the Father's love and has developed a passion for studying the Bible.

That deep devotion to God in turn has given her the desire to help others grow in their understanding of the love of God and to grow spiritually.